DEATH'S BETRAYAL

JANEAL FALOR

OTHER BOOKS BY JANEAL FALOR:

Death's Queen Series
Death's Queen (Death's Queen #1)
Death's Betrayal (Death's Queen #2)

Mine Series
Mine to Tarnish (Mine Prequel)
You Are Mine (Mine #1)
Mine to Spell (Mine #2)
Mine to Fear (Mine #3)
Sacrifice of Mine (Mine #4)

Darkening Light
Ever Darkening (Darkening Light #1)
Savage Light (Darkening Light #2)

Elven Princess
Bound by Birthright (Elven Princess #1)
Bound to Endure (Elven Princess #2)
Bound by Love (Elven Princess #3)

Standalone
Goddess Ascending
A Genie's Heart

To Erik
My world would be darker without you

CHAPTER 1

"Daros is missing," the guard says, voice cracking.

My sitting room seems to shrink in on me, shattering the pleasant morning. My throat locks up. My chest squeezes in on itself. "What do you mean, *missing?*"

When the guard doesn't speak right away, Nash says, "Tell us everything you know this instant."

The man glances at Nash and then at the floor. "He's gone from the dungeons. No one knows how."

My hands quiver. I slip one inside the other, to hide the trembling. This can't be happening. It can't. Despite my fear, I want to howl. To rage. How dare he escape? Why is he always above the law? Why does he get to escape punishment? "Have you put out a search for him?"

"Several people are looking for him, but we have not done an official search." The coward is backing away from me.

I jump to my feet, gritting my teeth. "Get on it. Now. And send me Jaku." He will answer for this.

"Yes, Your Majesty." The man bows and swiftly leaves the room.

Nash is at my side, reaching for me, but stops himself. "Are you all right?"

I don't answer. Can't. My eyes burn. I can't breathe. I'm showing too much weakness in front of him, but I can't stop it. I face the window, both to blink away the tears and to see if any threat is coming. Since I was attacked this way before, there are guards posted at it. It doesn't mean Daros won't find a sneakier approach. It would be like him to do so.

Why am I reacting this way? I can beat him. I did it before; I can do it again. Except he knows now that I won't kill him. It will give him more of a fighting chance. Not that he's heard of my vow not to kill, but I didn't do it when I could have. I didn't order his death, just his imprisonment.

All those times he tortured me and taught me I was worth less than nothing come back to me. If he manages to get a hold of me again... I clench my jaw. My whole body.

Nash's heat reaches me as he moves closer, although we're still not touching. "Ryn?"

The simple act of him saying my name stops the world from spinning. It doesn't stop the fear from clamping around my heart.

A moment later, there's a knock. Nash answers it. "Jaku, Head of the Guard, Your Highness."

I whip around. Jaku's normally tanned skin is pale. He's got ample muscles, despite being thick, but is it enough for him to go against Daros? I'm at least trained by Daros so I know him better. What do any of these men know about fighting him?

"What do you have to say for the loss of the prisoner?" I ask.

Jaku bows down on one knee. "Forgive me, Your Majesty. Place all the blame on me. It would appear he escaped sometime during the night. His loss was noticed when the watch changed earlier this morning and the guard who was supposed to be on duty was missing."

Somehow, I keep my legs strong. If only I could manage the rest of me to be so... I need to be so. I am so.

I take a steadying breath. This won't overcome me. I won't allow it. "Bring the guard who discovered them both missing to me."

"Yes, my lady." He stands and hurries from the room. I can't bring myself to look at his face—to see this reaction. I'm falling apart enough as it is without seeing him upset too.

I pick a chair in the corner of the room and plop down in it. It would be nice to grab a dagger as well, but I don't want Nash to see the terror clawing its way through me, making me into little bits of nothing, or the fury boiling in my chest. The two feelings are so strong and intertwined that they make me want to collapse.

"Ryn, tell me what you're thinking." Nash doesn't move. It's like he knows I can't handle myself, let alone him.

Daros.

He's coming.

The world tilts. I squish my eyelids closed. My chest feels as if it's collapsing in on itself. What will he do to me when he finds me? How will he punish me for not obeying him?

How much torture will I have to endure before death is a blissful release? Because I won't kill for him again. I won't give into his demands. I pull my anger out—use it to snuff my fear. It burns, searing through me.

Something brushes against my hand. I snatch it and twist.

"It's me." Nash's voice carries only a hint of worry. Of pain.

I drop his hand, still not looking at him. Not saying anything, though guilt plagues me. My throat is too clogged. I want to growl with a frenzy that's never captured me so heavily before.

"Ryn, you're scaring me." He doesn't sound scared. His voice is calm. Controlled. Smooth.

Everything I'm not.

Another knock sounds. A hiss of air escapes me. I sit up straight, staring mindlessly at nothing and pretending I have everything under control. No fear. No rage. Simply a queen doing her job.

When the door doesn't open, I say, "Answer it."

Nash does so. He says, "Your Majesty, it's Jaku Hanka Head of the Guard with Piru Nelta, the guard."

They both bow as they enter.

"What news do you have?" My words are disciplined.

They stay low. Jaku says to the floor, "Piru was on duty this morning and discovered the missing prisoner and guard."

"Rise. Tell me, Piru, what happened?"

"It's as Jaku said. I was on duty and went down to the dungeon. I was early so my partner wasn't there yet, and I didn't expect the other guards to be waiting for me. I thought he might have had troubles with one of the prisoners or something like that, so I searched the dungeon only to find the cell which held Daros to be empty. Neither of them were anywhere to be found, which is when I called attention to the problem."

And by that time, it was too late.

Nash says, "Do you think the guard with Daros acted on his own, or was he coerced?"

"Difficult to say," Jaku replies.

"What are we going to do so this doesn't happen again?" Nash asks.

"I'll do everything in my power to vet the guards more thoroughly," Jaku says. "To make sure there are more people on duty in the dungeon at a time. We thought there were enough, but there must be a secret tunnel Daros and the guard, Bolfa, were able to get through."

"And in the meantime, we have a prisoner and rogue guard on the loose?" I ask.

"I've sent men out to scout for them. We'll find them." Jaku shifts the tiniest bit.

"Send more. The best you have. And tell them he's extremely dangerous."

"I will, but may I advise you to leave the best guarding you here?"

Will it make a difference? If Daros wants me tortured, he'll have me. I shake away that thought. Let him come.

When I don't answer, Nash adds, "Please, Your Majesty."

"Fine. Send half, but I want results before this day is over."

"Yes, Your Highness," Jaku says. "I'll get right on that."

"Keep me updated." I wave him off.

They slip from the room. Nash is in front of me, kneeling on the ground and staring up at me with his hazel eyes with specks of blue. "Please talk to me. Let me help you."

Daros could make me do terrible things. A worse thought enters my mind—what if he harms those around me?

My stomach roils. I jump to my feet, and Nash scrambles out of the way. I run to my bedroom and throw up in my wash basin.

Terror sluices through me. I dry heave.

I focus on breathing, like Daros taught me to do, to control myself. Three short breaths. It had to come from him. Everything comes from him. Nothing can happen in my life without him somehow being involved. The only thing he never expected was for me to become queen. When I did, he was certain he could control me. That I would give way under his threats to tell everyone I killed the last queen.

I had him arrested instead, three weeks ago, and I thought that'd be the end of it. I thought he'd rot in prison.

I should have known better.

When my stomach decides it's had enough, I lean back. Nash puts a glass of water in front of me. I swish the water through my mouth and spit it out.

"What's going through your mind?" he asks. "How can I help? Please… I'll do anything you need. You haven't told me much about Daros, but I know he was bad. There's more in the past than either you or he have said. But I care about you. I don't want this to eat you up inside. Let me assist in any way I can."

No one can. Daros is my burden alone, and no one else should have to deal with him.

5

I'm the queen now. Despite that, I'm more alone than I ever was before. I have to figure out a way around this, but I don't know how.

I put my back against the wall and look out my window. Nash reaches for my hand and skin brushes against skin. He's warm. Soothing. Feels oh so good, and after all this time of having no one, I feel like I've earned it. Like I deserve a little happiness. But there's one problem.

"Don't," I lash out. "You know we can't touch. That the law forbids it." The unbreakable law I can do nothing about.

He snakes his hand back, like I stabbed it with my poisoned dagger. "Sorry. I wanted to comfort you."

I ache for it, yet I know there's no reassurance when Daros is after me. Nor is there sweetness with a law that forbids it. "Leave."

"I'm sorry?"

"Leave *now*," I yell.

His arms fall slack at his sides. He takes a step back. And then another. Not fast enough. I want to push him away. Save him from being associated with my Daros-tainted self. But it's too late. He's my Head Advisor. Daros knows he's connected to me. I can only keep distance between us and hope that's enough.

I can't let Daros figure out how much Nash does mean to me. "*Go.*"

He stares at me a moment, eyes wide, and then rushes from the bedroom. A moment later, the door to my sitting room slams closed.

What have I done?

CHAPTER 2

THE COUNCIL ROOM is filled to the brim with reigning members and their assistants. It's been an hour since Nash left my room, but now he's next to me. Normally, that'd bring me comfort. Today, it brings worry.

The council members are noisily chatting away when they're not giving me sidelong glances followed by quick head-ducks. I'm not in the mood for their antics today. Not in the mood for anything but running.

I'm the queen of this country; I can't run away.

It's a depressing thought.

"Quiet." Nash brings things to order.

If only I could send him to some other place, where he'd be safe. Just sitting next to him is making me nervous. I lean away.

He continues when the room quiets down. "We have pressing business to attend. The criminal Daros, who tried to kill the queen, set up other queens' deaths, and committed many other atrocities, has escaped."

There are a few gasps, but most have probably heard the rumors.

Yuka, Head of Arts, turns to Jaku. "How could this have happened?"

"Due to lack of evidence of a struggle, we think there was a rogue guard. We're doing everything we can to prevent this from happening in the future, including—but not limited to—having more than two guards on duty at a time."

"What happened to the other guard?" Timit asks.

"He was knocked unconscious," Jaku says. "After that, there was no sighting of either Bolfa or Daros. We assume they used a secret tunnel."

Like the secret tunnel Daros told me about, that I used to access Queen Deedra's chambers and kill her. I should have realized he'd know more about how to get around. Should have put extra men on him. Should have had him executed when I had the chance. Never mind that I promised myself never to kill again, I should have done it anyway.

Now, I'm faced with the consequences.

Everyone is talking over one another. They probably have been for some time.

"*Silence.*" My voice carries over their noise, quieting them. "One at a time. We will be civil about this."

Because that's all I have left. That and my fury.

They look at me, hushing their tongues. I'm grateful it worked. "I need ideas on how we can find the prisoner. If you don't have anything useful to offer, stay silent. Time is of the essence, and we've lost too much of it. Jaku, Head of the Guard, and Sidle, Head of Military, are most likely to have useful input, so they will speak first."

Sidle shakes his head. "Forgive me, Your Majesty, but the military is almost non-existent. I'm more of a figurehead than anything."

"Why is it so small?"

He looks down. "Because we don't fight with other countries. The mountains surrounding our country have always been

8

enough to keep them away, and our people have been well-behaved, any issues contained by the guard."

I want to growl at the absurdity. "You can't have gotten into this position without knowing something about how to deal with an escapee. Give me information I can use. Now."

"It's impossible to track him, since we don't know which secret tunnel we presume he used. We know of none in the dungeons, but Jaku has men looking for them."

"Jaku?" I ask.

"We've found no secret tunnels yet. I do have men out combing the streets and looking in bars and nearby establishments. We'll find them."

It's not the guard I'm worried about; it's Daros. "Words are pretty, but not enough to save a life. I need thoughts. Ideas. Ways to get things moving." To get him found. When no one speaks up, I huff. "I'm wasting my time having a council meeting."

"It's not that we don't want to help, Your Highness. We don't know where to look for him," Sidle says.

But I do.

Why didn't I realize this sooner? It isn't that I want to go, but if I don't more people than just myself will be in peril. This is something I must do. Not even facing my worst fears can stop me. I jump to my feet. Everyone else does, some stumbling to do so, but I barely notice. One thought has taken hold of me. "I know where to find him. Jaku, you're with me. Grab your best guards. We're heading out within ten minutes."

I storm out of the room and head for the halls, like Daros himself is after me.

Multiple footsteps are following. The way behind me is filled with noise, but I ignore it. I have to focus if I'm going to do this. It's my one chance. I have to give it my best.

When I get to my sitting room, so I can change clothes and arm myself better, my guard Wilric says, "Let me check your rooms first."

"Make it quick."

He hurries off, and I tap my foot. I can't bring myself to look at Nash. It's still too painful to think of what I may have done to him by letting Daros escape. I may have risked more than his life. More than my own. More than those of others around me.

I can't show a partiality to him now, when others are near. Daros knows everything, no matter how hard I try to hide it. If he figures out a way to use my feelings for my people against me, I don't know what I'll do.

It won't come to that. We'll go to his house, find him, and I will give him a death sentence, despite what promises I made.

Wilric returns. "Your rooms are clear, my lady."

I zip in, go past the sitting room, and straight to the bedroom. I've a plethora of daggers and poisons on my person, but it's not enough if I'm to take down Daros. I grab the rest of my tools. The poisons won't do any good, since he's either immune to them or has antidotes, but I grab them anyway.

I change to my best outfit for the occasion—a pair of black pants with multiple pockets for daggers and weapons. Then I put on a purple tunic with a black belt that has more places for weapons. Both are designed to give me freedom of movement.

So much better than a dress.

I halt long enough to glance out the window. I want to sleep and dream of the First Queen. Her advice would be soothing now, if nothing else.

I march through my rooms, and my escorts gather around me. "We are going to Daros's house," I say. "You will follow my orders exactly. Wilric, run and see if Jaku is ready. Nash, you're staying here."

Wilric takes off before I've finished. Nash is just as quick to reply, "I'm going."

"It's not safe for us both to go. If I should fall, we'll need someone to run the country until another queen is chosen."

"I was a guard before I was your Head Advisor. I've trained for this and continue to do so. I can help."

I wish I could express my fears, but there are too many people around. Even if it was only Nash, I can't let this out. Can't voice my fears and have them become more real than they already are.

I stare him down. He stares right back.

"Jaku is ready, Your Majesty." Wilric pulls my attention away from Nash. "He will meet us at the front gates."

"Head out." I ignore Nash. Maybe if I do so the entire time we're out, Daros won't pick up on my feelings toward him.

He seems to be good with this, as he takes a spot at my side. I pretend to pay him no mind. It's hard when my body hums awareness at his very presence, but I try. My escorts continue to surround me as we go through the maze of hallways toward the front entrance. The path is familiar to me now, though there are still parts of the palace I don't know.

The closer we get to the front gates, the more my skin prickles. The more I want to turn back. But I refuse to stand down when this may be the only chance to catch him.

When we finally get to the gate, I'm pleased to see Jaku has a plethora of guards with him. More so than I've ever seen in one place before.

This is it. I can do this. Daros will fall.

I shout out directions to the soldiers as we move through the portcullis and down the lane. "Everyone needs to stay with a partner. This man is cunning and dangerous. When we get there, I want absolute silence. We will encircle his house before anyone enters."

"What about your safety, Your Majesty?" Jaku asks.

"Getting Daros is your first priority. If it makes you feel better, a few men can stay close to me." Not that I want to be hampered by them.

"Afet, Eldim, Wilric, and I will stay with the queen," he says. "The rest of you follow her orders."

The men come to me. They give me just enough room to walk, but not an inch more. Nash needs to stay out of danger's way. Which he won't if my life is at risk.

None of them will.

It's a startling realization. There may be people who want me dead, but there are others who will defend me until the very end. At some point, my life became worth more than I ever thought it could. Than Daros ever told me it would.

I am worth something.

The thought puts a grin on my face—one that's tempered by the situation but still wide.

The houses grow nicer as we pass into the Kurah area. Cleaner. More put together. The road is a smooth cobblestone. It hasn't been that long since I ran past all the houses, chased by one of Daros's men. Only, that time, I was by myself and hadn't a clue what I was doing. This time I do.

I'm taking him down.

I motion for silence as we near the house. When it comes into view, my stomach flops. Up, high on the ridge, is the window to my old bedroom. The one I escaped through.

The closer we get, the more my body revolts—skin prickling, hands clammy, mouth dry.

I don't want to do this.

I'm going to.

But not without my weapons. I take a dagger in each hand.

As soon as we reach the building, I motion for the group to move around it. They move silently and swiftly. Much more so than I expected. Once the signal that they're in place comes from the back around to the soldiers in the front, I stride toward the door.

"Let me go in first, Your Majesty." Jaku doesn't wait for me to respond. He and Wilric go ahead of me.

Jaku slips the door open, while several men point their crossbows at it, in case anyone should come out. The fact that it wasn't locked isn't a good sign. Is Daros in there waiting for us with a group of his men? Waiting for me? No matter that it hasn't been long—knowing Daros, he has a whole slew of assassins at his beck and call.

I clutch my daggers tighter than I should, but I can't help it.

Nash is at my side. Even if I can't see him out of the corner of my eye, I can feel his presence. His warmth.

As I walk in after Jaku and Wilric, Nash is on my heels, with his sword drawn. Doing my best to ignore him—which is next to impossible—I slink through the house. There are no sounds. No people. No hint of life.

We should have run into someone on watch by now, if not more than one. Where is everyone? The house is crawling with my guards now. They're everywhere I turn. I go up the curving stairs. The last time I was here, I felt utter despair, but was determined to get away and never kill again.

I nudge open the door of my old room.

"Let me go first," Nash says.

But I'm already in.

It's as I left it. Bare. There's nothing here except a couple of blankets.

I flex my fingers over the handle of my dagger. Memories fly at me—Daros choking me, dunking me in water until I couldn't breathe, breaking me and molding me into who he wanted me to be...

"Are you all right?" Nash's voice is barely above a whisper as he moves deeper into the room.

Am I?

"Ryn?"

"This was my room." The words tumble from me. "The whole time he raised me, I lived here." I remember believing there were monsters in the corners when I was little. None were as scary as the monster that haunted my days, though.

He glances around, probably taking in the small area again with new eyes. "Did he move the furniture out?"

"There never was any." My voice sounds dead. I step back, so I'm next to the entrance.

His eyebrows mush together before rising up high. "Why wouldn't he give you furniture? A bed, at the very least?"

I don't answer. Can't.

He takes a step toward me. There's a soft creak of someone on the stairs.

Daros, coming to wrap his hands around my throat.

I bring my blade up to the neck of the person coming inside the room. The blade presses into their skin. He holds still as can be.

It's not Daros I'm holding a weapon to; it's Jaku. I snake back my arm. "Sorry."

There's a thin line of red where the blade was. He touches it, and his fingers come away wet with blood. I suppose I was a little too forceful, but that's what this place does to me. I have to be prepared for Daros, though it's evident he's not wandering the house. There's always a chance, no matter how small.

To his credit, Jaku doesn't comment on it. He dabs at the wound with a handkerchief from his pocket and says, "The house is clear. There are no signs of life."

I nod. There's one area I'm sure they haven't checked.

I motion Jaku down the stairs, before Nash and I follow after him. I move like a cat, prowling through the house with light steps. If Daros is in the hidden room, I don't want to meet him there. Not in that place.

What other choice do I have?

I'm on edge, memories of tiptoeing around flooding me, but my guards offer some comfort. Just not the kind I expected. Especially since it was a guard who betrayed me and let Daros free. I suppose the men and women who watch over me are to be trusted more than the ones on duty in the dungeons since they've been around longer and put through more testing. But is there any way to know their loyalty is sure?

The dark wood of the walls adds to the heaviness in my chest. The rugs over the same dark floor soften my footsteps. When we reach the outside of Daros's personal office, there's a stain of blood on the rug.

My blood.

He backhanded me with rings on when I didn't obey him fast enough, sending me flying to the floor, dripping red everywhere.

I'm furious yet scared, and I don't have a way to stop it. Doesn't matter. If Daros is in his hidden room, I'm not sure how I'll react. I don't want to fight him again. Yet there's no way I can let him go without a fight.

The door is wide open, the hidden room concealed inside. With slow, steady breaths, I try to get my shaking under control.

"Are we looking for something, Your Majesty?" Jaku's voice comes from behind me.

At some point he went from leading to following. My memories of this house make it hard to pay attention; it's a deadly trait that may get me killed.

I press on, not saying anything. I wasn't supposed to talk in here unless Daros commanded it, and I've already said too much.

I step inside. It's not like I remember it. The piles of papers on the desk are gone, books missing from his shelves. Chairs are knocked over, and the desk is shifted toward the single window. Did my guards do this, or was it Daros's people? Either way, he's not here.

Unless he's in *the* room.

I walk over to the empty bookshelf. To move all this stuff away must have taken some time. How long did he have to empty it? Did he do this even before he was captured? I can't imagine him ruining his things if he thought he was going to win me over at the coronation ball.

Of course, I wasn't ever coronated. This still needs remedying, along with lowering the taxes, making the tax collection system better, and many other law changes.

I reach to the far side of the bookshelf and flick the hidden lever that's smaller than my finger. I've had to flick it many times before.

Everything in me screams to run the other way.

My eyes burn.

My heart aches.

The soft whisk of the secret door opening is loud in the silent room. I don't turn to see who's following. I have to face this alone.

I go in before anyone can stop me, because it's the only way I'm going to make it. I keep my daggers out, ready for any attack that may come my way.

The only light comes from the coals in the fireplace. Either someone is here or they were recently, if the fire hasn't gone all the way out.

Footsteps come after me as I stand frozen several steps inside. My feet won't move. My momentum is gone. I want to vomit.

Someone's breathing is ragged. Harsh.

It's my own.

The room brightens. At first, all I can see is Jaku, holding a torch by the fireplace. Then the light wavers over the room. The vat of oil by the fireplace. The tub of water. The chains on the walls.

I shrink back.

Nash hisses. Other people murmur. Jaku moves his torch around the room, making me take everything in even more in depth. My daggers almost fall from my hands, but I tighten my grip.

It's then I see the dark shape in the middle of the floor. Daros? No. It's male but too thin. I can't make much else out, since he's lying on his stomach. I prepare my weapons to attack should this person jump up. Nash keeps his sword at the ready as he inches past me. He bends down and seeks the man's pulse.

A moment later, he says, "Dead."

"Who is it?" Jaku asks.

Both men glance my way but say nothing further.

Nash rolls the man over.

Jaku grunts. "Bolfa. The guard who let Daros escape."

I hope the poor man didn't pay for his choice of helping Daros by spending too long in this room of horrors.

Jaku moves forward. He leans down when he gets to Bolfa's remains. "There's something pinned to his shirt."

Nash takes it off. It's a piece of paper. He holds it up to the light and grimaces.

"What does it say?" I try to make my voice commanding, but it comes out small. Rickety.

With a quick glance at me, he folds the paper in half.

"What does it say?" My words are stronger this time.

Jaku nods at Nash.

With a scowl, Nash holds out the paper to me. I open it up. The handwriting is familiar, even if I wasn't supposed to read it growing up. But now I'm supposed to. This note is meant for no one but me.

YOU WILL PAY.

I SWALLOW. "HE'S NOT HERE."

"The body is cold, Your Highness," Jaku says. "Judging by that and the fire's coals, I'd say it's been since sometime this morning that someone was here."

"We missed him." Nash sighs.

Daros is still out there hunting me.

Being in this room makes me want to cower. To hide. But no more. I will not be his tool to be used out of fear.

Something burns deep inside my gut. A vicious anger, like molten lava boiling through my veins.

With a growl, I hurl my knife at the far wall. It sticks in the wood, wobbling. Just like my heart.

Doesn't matter. I will find him, and I will have him put to death.

CHAPTER 3

THE ENSUING SCRAMBLE TO find anything of use in Daros's home is fruitless. Jaku leaves a few people behind, to take care of the body. The rest of us march back to the palace.

Nash stays close by. I wonder what he's thinking. If he's disgusted by me.

I am.

But mostly, I'm worried.

The anger has burned off and left me with little to hold onto. I need something, but I don't know what. I want Daros recaptured, so I don't have to fear the things he can do to me or those around me. It's too much to deal with. My brain is overloaded, so I turn off my feelings.

Let myself be numb.

I take note of everything going through the portcullis, into the palace, through the halls, and to my rooms. There are guards everywhere, which should make me feel safe but only leads me to wonder which of them will betray me.

Nash opens the door to my sitting room, says something I can't hear to Jaku follows me into the room.

I take quick stock of both rooms. When I find nothing, I return to the sitting room, to find Nash watching me with a wary gaze.

I'm still holding a dagger in each hand.

I put them away. "Did you need something?"

He straightens. "I was wondering if there is anything further you would like us to do, besides the search we have going on for Daros."

I flinch at the sound of his name. Everything is too close to the surface. "I don't know."

Nash takes a step toward me, stops, and backtracks. "If you think of anything, please let me know. I want him captured."

As do I.

He bows and leaves the room. Something about those gestures seems odd. I don't know what, just that it leaves me unsettled. I head to my bedroom, and moments later, my servant and friend, Inkga, joins me.

"I heard about what happened," she says. "I'm sorry he got away."

I clench my jaw. I don't want to tune her out. To be rude. What else can I do, though? I want nothing to do with reminders of him, but they are everywhere.

Crushing.

Blinding.

Suffocating.

"My Lady, are you all right?"

I give a heavy blink. "Fine. Let's just get ready for bed."

While I change, she cleans up around my room even though it's pretty much too clean. As soon as I got clothes I could put on myself, I insisted she no longer help me with them. It seems silly to have someone else dress me.

Once I'm ready and she's finished turning down the bed, she says, "There are extra guards outside your window and in the hall. Please don't hesitate to let me know if you need anything. Good night."

I nod, though I have no intention of needing a thing from her or the guards. She curtseys and leaves. Immediately, I want her back. The room is darker. Colder.

I climb in bed, holding the blankets around me tight. I'm not sure I can sleep, but I'm in no mood for climbing to the roof. I brush my hand under my pillow where I stashed a couple of daggers. That's more reassuring than anything else tonight. If only I didn't need to use them. I've been attacked in my rooms far too much, as it is.

That's not all that's under here, though. The doll the little girl gave me at the ball is here as well. I take it out and hug it close before putting it back. She gave up something special to her, to give it to me. I wonder how she is. If she has enough to eat. If the supplies I sent her family helped.

I keep my grip tight around my dagger as I try to drift off. There are guards on the ground outside my window and sitting room. I should be safe from *him*. Still, I can't let go of my dagger.

I relax my grip and ease my arm away it. The blades are there; this has to be enough. It's always been enough.

But not now.

I toss and turn for far too long. I want to climb down on the floor but can't bring myself to get up. Finally, the night fades and the colors blossom.

The colors of the sunset are softer than I usually dream, but still there, as is the First Queen, who sits nearby. I take in her typical green dress, her green eyes, the matching green-jeweled necklace, and long blonde hair. I wouldn't think one person could be so comforting, but her presence is. It's strong and true. Patient and calm. Everything I need in this minute.

"You've had a hard setback," she says.

"Nothing I can't handle."

"You don't have to pretend with me. I know these things. Why don't you have a seat?"

I remain standing and shift from one leg to the other.

"You did a good job standing up to him in the first place. And then, when he came to the ball and outed you for being an assassin who killed the last queen before trying to kill you, you were so brave. Even in the face of what he made you do to poor Deedra, you championed for what's right and good. You held your ground." She sounds so sure of herself.

"You don't understand," I say.

"Then tell me. I want to know."

I don't want to talk about it. I don't say it out loud, but she's in my head; she reads my thoughts.

"But you need to."

I huff.

"Come on, now. There's no reason to be like this. It really does help to talk about it. I promise."

I still don't want to, but since she can read my mind anyway, there's no use fighting it. "He hurt me, for all my life. He did whatever he wanted to me. He used me to do his dirty work. Trained me to kill whoever he wanted gone. I knew there was more to life, but I didn't know I could have it. When I escaped from him, it was so freeing."

"And then he found you."

I give in and sit. It's a strange feeling, not sitting on anything, but typical for a dream maybe. "He found me and did what I feared—he told everyone what I was."

"That hasn't been so bad for you."

"Only because the people fear my guards. Fear me." Mostly me, the Shadow Wraith.

"You don't want to be feared?"

I take a moment to think about it. "Does a good queen want to be feared?"

"That's up to you to decide."

"But I thought you were here to guide me?"

"I am, and I will. But some things are better learned on your own."

I glare at her, wishing she'd give me the answers. "I know that the people—my people—haven't been coming around to my way of thinking. Of course they weren't before, either. Maybe I need to be officially coronated and moved into my duties with them. Maybe then they will come to respect me, instead of being scared. I have to swear to do better."

"It sounds like a wise plan."

A coronation, then. I should set that in motion.

"You know, you shouldn't worry about Daros coming back, when you defeated him once."

"Who says I'm worried?"

"It's there, in your thoughts, unguarded."

I cross my arms. "So what if I am? I have every reason to fear him. Beating him was a fluke. There's no telling I could ever do that again. Though this time I won't be alone, neither will he. Besides, he controlled me almost my entire life. What's to stop that now? He may not come after me, but someone will. I will pay for what I've done."

"You need to move on. To live your life."

I'm silent, trying to keep my thoughts away from her soft touch.

She sighs. "Please move on with your life, though it's hard. The coronation is a good idea. You should do it." When I don't respond, she says, "It's all right to have a weakness. Everyone does."

"What's yours, then?"

She looks down. "Mine doesn't matter. I'm no longer living a real life. I'm simply guiding you."

Can it be true? Is it okay to have a weakness? To have a soft spot for something? For myself and my people?

"You know it is. Be true to yourself."

Her words stir something in my heart that I'm not sure I'm ready to face. "You're not mad at me for killing Queen Deedra?" I ask.

"No, dearest. It came from Daros, not you. It was not your choice to be the Shadow Wraith. He forced you into it. Now that you've seen the light, you've left that persona behind. You have to forgive yourself for the part you played in it."

Maybe.

"No maybe about it. But no matter what I tell you, you'll have to believe it for yourself."

I sigh. I wish things were easier.

"I do, as well."

This makes me think of something we haven't talked about in the past few weeks. Why could I feel her presence during my fight with Daros, when I captured him?

"Because of the Mortum Tura. I told you, the more you drink it, the stronger you will become. The more connected we'll be."

I don't know how I feel about that.

"You don't have to decide now, but I must go. We'll talk more soon," she says.

"I'll think about what you said."

"That's all I can ask."

Will it help, or will it be my undoing?

CHAPTER 4

THE MORNING IS bright and cheery. I'm not.

It's still early, and Inkga has yet to arrive, so I dress. I concentrate on concealing weapons and on what the First Queen said. I can't handle all of it. But the part about setting the coronation in motion and helping my people? That I can do. I should have done it right after the first failed attempt on my life, but I was too busy trying to undo the damage Daros did by telling everyone who I am.

After the ball, the people shunned me. They still shun me, in truth. They're scared of the Shadow Wraith, coming to destroy them now as their queen, instead of an unknown assassin. Despite that, I've been trying to meet with them, to ease their fears with kindness. Most still quiver before me.

I hurry through my rooms to where Nash is waiting along with some guards. I want to ask him how long he's been here. How much sleep he's gotten. What he's thinking. But I don't want to be more familiar than I already am. Not when I'm so worried for him. For all of us.

"Your Majesty." He bows at me, as do the other guards, one at a time so they have someone always watching the hall.

"I would like you to arrange some things for me," I say. "If you will step in here, we can discuss it."

"Certainly." He follows me in.

I take a seat in the corner, where I can watch both the entrance and the window. It's something I'd normally do but now feels even more imperative.

The coronation would take time to put together, but there is something else I could do to make the people happy. To make me happy.

"I have some things I'd like you to help with," I say.

I should talk to Timit about it first, though I've talked to him about it a little in the past. He's always so hesitant—doesn't want money going anywhere but to him. I may as well go ahead with it and deal with the consequences later. I should also give a decree, but I'd rather do it myself. I want my people to hear from my own mouth what I'm doing for them so there's no mistaking it.

"Go ahead." His words are stiff. Formal.

I don't like it at all, but I brought it on myself. "I would like to have a meeting with as many citizens as you can get together this afternoon. I need to tell them about a new law." What I should have told them. I was to lower taxes at the ball, but it never happened. It's far past time to do so.

"I can arrange that. I can't guarantee many people will be there on such short notice, but I'll do what I can. Where would you like them to gather?"

"The throne room or ballroom. Which do you think is better?"

"If it's official business, the throne room. Otherwise, the ballroom."

"The throne room, then."

"It will be done."

"Good. And for the other business—I would like you to arrange a coronation, since it was canceled at the ball. You can enlist the ladies-in-waiting or anyone else you'd like. The Head of Relations with the Queen can help."

He nods. "I'll make sure it is. When did you want to hold it?"

"Let's say one week from today. If that's not a problem."

"That's soon, but I'll take care of it."

"Thank you." I want to say more—tell him my thoughts, feelings, and fears—but I don't dare. It was hard enough talking to the First Queen about them. I don't want to speak about them anymore.

"Are you all right?" He sounds more like himself than he has the whole time he's been here.

"Fine." The word cracks, betraying me.

He narrows his eyes. I know he doesn't believe me, but will he ask?

He stands. "If that is all, Your Majesty, I will get it in order."

I relax back into my chair, uncertain if I'm glad he is ignoring my response. "That is all."

"I will report when I have news." He bows.

I watch him walk. I miss his realness. His charm. The kiss we shared and have avoided mentioning since.

It should have never taken place, but I ache for its comforting reassurance. For the warmth that came with it. The nearness. The connection.

Pushing the feelings aside, I walk out into the hall, to find my guards waiting like always. Wilric, Eldim, Stird, and Afet—I'm getting better at keeping track of them. There are still a lot of guards whose names I don't know, though, including a few women who are helping today.

I hurry to the corridor, where I run into Inkga.

"You're ready, my lady," she says. "Should I have breakfast sent up?"

"Please do. Enough for my ladies-in-waiting. I'll eat later, so we don't have to worry about poison meant for me getting mixed into one of their plates." After Inkga being poisoned when I was supposed to be, I can't chance it happening again. "Once you have that going, will you please let the ladies know I would like to meet with all of them in my sitting room?"

"Of course. Anything else, Your Highness?"

Egh. They still call me these names much too often. But I don't want them to stop now with Daros on the loose. I don't want to show familiarity with anyone. All my life, he's known everything about me, except for when I decided to run. Maybe because that was a spur of the moment decision, he didn't have time to learn it. The people I care about, though? There's plenty of time to learn about them. What would I do if he took Inkga away from me? She's much too sweet to have to deal with his form of punishment.

"No, that will be all," I say.

I slip back in my room and settle in my chair to wait. It takes much too long. I tap my foot on the ground, wanting to pace, but not wanting to show nerves, even if my room is empty of people.

Something flashes out of the corner of my eye. I whip to the side, daggers drawn.

No one is there.

I swallow and try to quiet my pounding heart. Daros isn't here. None of his men are here. I'm safe. My people are safe.

For now.

Who knows how long it'll last?

A knock sounds.

"Enter," I say, not caring that I have no one here to answer it for me.

The ladies-in-waiting pile in the room—all twelve of them. The thirteenth one, Faya—the grandmotherly lady I trusted—is now in the dungeons. I still can't believe she was behind the plot with Ranen and Borkus to take my life.

They curtsy, and I tell them to be seated. Jem sits farthest from me, though I can see her dainty mole above her lip and to the right. Having her back to the window is a bad choice, but that's her decision. The rest settle around in various chairs. It's then I realize I don't know most of their names. I've been remiss.

Time to fix that.

"Before we start, I would like each of you to say your first name. No *Your Highness, Your Majesty,* or *my lady.* Just your first name." And I'll try to remember them.

They look at me with rounded eyes. Why, I'm not sure, so I choose to ignore it. I nod for the first one—a girl several years older than me, with the typical brown hair, grey eyes, and a tight smile—to go ahead.

"I'm Suyla of Trentin," she says.

"Thank you, Suyla. No need to say where you are from, though."

She nods, and the next woman speaks.

"Lipla." She looks to be in her thirties and has golden skin, which reminds me that I know her from before.

"Freza." She's in her late twenties and has a light dusting of freckles across her fair skin.

"Pina." Her voice is dainty, though she's the biggest of the group. She looks younger than me, but not by much.

The next girl, I remember, with her golden hair and eyes, and her loyalty to Jem. "I'm Inyi," she says.

"Jem." There's a snide quality to Jem's voice, but I ignore it; it's always been there. Besides, it's not as bad as it used to be.

They continue around the room, but I have a hard time concentrating. I'll ask their names again if I need them. *When* I need them. I'm determined to utilize them more than I have previously.

When the last one finishes, I say, "Thank you. In case you don't know why we're meeting, I've asked my Head Advisor to arrange my coronation for one week from today. You are to be included in the preparations."

They beam, except for Jem, who stays expressionless.

"How may we help, Your Majesty?" Inyi asks.

It was nice, losing the title. For a moment, anyway. "In any way my Head Advisor asks you to. I'm sure he'll hand over most details to you. It should take place in the throne room and have a mixture of classes there. I don't want to cater to just the upper class."

"We can do that, Your Highness," Pina says, joy folding through her words.

"Excellent. Do you have any other questions?" I ask.

They stay silent. I suppose they trained for this. I would have nothing but questions, but since I put them in charge, I'll leave them to it.

"Good. One more thing. I am making an announcement this afternoon. Afterward, and for the next couple of days, I want you to go out among the people of Poruah, Medi, and Kurah class and figure out how they feel about it. You ladies are to be my eyes and ears."

I have to trust them with this; there's no one else to do it. The guards I can count on are taking turns protecting me and sleeping. Normally, I wouldn't think I needed protection, but with Daros on the loose, anything can happen. Messengers or servants would work, but I'm not putting Inkga in harm's way, and she's the only one I know. I can read people I know better than those I don't, and I know my ladies-in-waiting a little. I should, after all the time I've spent listening to them prattle.

"Forgive me, my queen," Freza says. "We aren't accustomed to such tasks."

"It's time to become accustomed to them. This won't be your last."

She raises her eyebrows, but she says nothing further.

"Anyone else?" I scan the room, taking in their reactions. Most are like Freza, but Jem is straight-faced, appearing indifferent. "I expect a report from each of you in a couple days. You are dismissed."

They stand and curtsy. A few give backward glances, but most shuffle away. Once they are all gone, I give a sigh of relief.

Handling others is stressful. I don't know what to do with them. How to act.

There is one good thing, though—for a moment there, I forgot about Daros. Maybe this is the key. Serve my people; let my worries slide away.

If only it was enough.

CHAPTER 5

After Inkga helps me change into more formal clothing,—a dress, *ugh*—I head to the throne room. During the coronation, I'll have to walk the length of the huge room, but today, we wind through the hallways toward the back of the room.

Several guards are with me, along with the council that fell in line behind me at some point. I glance back and see Nash leading them. I turn back around before we can make eye contact. Before I do something I'll later regret, like throwing myself in his arms and sobbing. That wouldn't do.

We come to the door, and the council filters past me to find their places to stand—according to their rank, no doubt. Nash doesn't even look at me as he goes by. The only one who makes any comments toward me is Yuka, my Head of Arts. She says, "I'm anxious to see what you're going to tell everyone, Your Majesty."

I nod to her, and she continues on. We'll see if she's just as anxious when she hears I'm lowering taxes for the Poruah and Medi.

After the council is in, Wilric peeks his head in the room. "The crowd is ready for you, Your Highness."

"Thank you."

"Her Majesty, Queen Ryn," a male voice calls out.

I enter the room and hold in a gasp at the amount of people gathered.

They're everywhere, crammed together in the huge space. There must be at least a thousand. Maybe more. All to hear my announcement. Those in the back won't hear me well, though.

"The Shadow Wraith isn't my queen," a female voice yells.

Though I fear she's right, I ignore her. Not being the queen means being dead, which isn't an option.

I make my way over to the throne on the dais, the only piece of furniture in the room. I stand in front of it, not wanting to sit, despite my terror threatening to creep its way into me. Someone sent by Daros is probably in this crowd right now. They can't make it to me. My escorts are lined up in front of everyone, and more line the wall behind me.

That doesn't hold much comfort, not if they have a projectile weapon.

But no more wasting time. I can do this. "My people." The room quiets. Every gaze is focused on me. I can even make out those in the back.

"I have news I want to share with you." May as well get right to it; I was never good at making speeches. I wasn't supposed to talk. "I am lowering the taxes for the Poruah and Medi class by half. To combat this, I'm raising them for the Kurah class by a quarter."

The room is a cacophony. Gasps and hisses. Cheers and growls. The Kurah may hate me now, but I don't regret it. The Poruah needed this. I needed this.

I don't know what to do now. The noise is too much. People seem to be talking to each other as much as they are talking to me, though I can't hear them.

I glance at Nash. He's smiling.

That little expression made this worth it.

There's nothing else for me to do. I turn and leave the room.

The door closes, taking out most of the noise. The guards nod at me, and I lead the way back to my room.

It feels good to do something for my people. Really do something. Now to figure out what else I should be doing for them.

* * *

It's been a day since I lowered taxes, and I'm still thinking about what the First Queen said. Is it really okay to have a weakness? I don't know.

There's a knock. Lunch is here. "Enter."

Nash strides in. My pulse speeds up. Seeing him is like an adrenaline rush.

He gives a stiff bow. "I wanted to know if you had anything for me to do, Your Majesty. I've got people working on the coronation for next week. It should turn out well."

I grin. Daros's escape doesn't matter. Now that my panic has worn off, I know he can't see into my room. Into my heart. "Please have a seat."

He takes the chair Jem sat in, farthest from me. He must be upset.

I wonder again about that softness I need to have. The ability to trust others. Can I say what I need to? Can I do it? I care enough about Nash to try.

"I'm sorry." The words feel like they're choking out of me.

Nash's eyes are wide. "What was that?"

"I'm sorry I've been rude to you. That I haven't been communicating better."

He stares a moment. "It's fine."

"No, it's not. I was scared of Daros"—still am—"I didn't know how to respond. I'm…not used to letting people in."

Without hesitation, he moves to the chair next to mine. "Please don't think about it again. After seeing his house and…everything

34

in it, I can't imagine how you must feel. How terrifying this must all be for you."

I don't say anything. Can't. Despite my panic lessening, it's stuck in my gut with my fear, roiling about like a monster let loose.

My lunch arrives, and Nash lets the servant in. She sets a tray on the low table in front of me. "Do you need anything else, Your Majesty?"

"No, thank you. Wait. Yes. Would you please bring up a tray for Nash?"

"I'd be happy to." With a curtsy, she leaves.

"You didn't have to do that," Nash says.

"I'm not about to eat while you sit and watch. Though I do worry. Last time I asked them to bring more food, Faya tried to poison me and instead poisoned Inkga." And killed someone to allay suspicion.

"We've tightened security, and no one has tried for your life in a week. I think I'll be all right."

"Still." I grab the plate of roast chicken and vegetables off my tray and smell it before tasting it. "This is fine. And now yours." I hand it to him.

He doesn't take it. "I can't eat it. It belongs to you."

"Not anymore. I know it's safe."

With a sigh, he takes it. "You know, I really should be tasting your food for you, not the other way around. Or hire a tester for you."

I just grin at him.

"I'll eat this when your food comes." He sets the plate back down and clears his throat. "Thank you for trusting me again."

I nod, chest tightening.

"We'll find him."

Daros. "Not if he doesn't want to be found."

"How can you be so certain?" Nash asks.

"Because I lived with him my whole life."

He raises his eyebrows. "Your entire life?"

"Yes." The word comes out fainter than I meant it to.

He reaches out like he's going to take my hand before jerking his arm back. "I can't imagine what that must have been like."

"Not good." I lean forward and take his hand. He might not want to hold mine, but I need the contact. He tries to pull away, but I stop him. "Are you pulling away because you don't like me?" I ask.

"How could you think that? No. I'm pulling away because of the law. I'm not supposed to touch you."

No one is. "I don't care. No one's here. No one can see. I want to touch you." Need to.

"We shouldn't." But his voice is wavering.

"Please." That word hardly ever comes out of me. "No one ever comforts me. At least give me this little bit."

He pulls away again, and this time I let him, a tear ripping through my heart. Until he stands, bends down, and wraps his arms around me. It can't be a comfortable position for him, but for me, it's perfect.

It makes me close my eyes, to revel in his arms. His warmth. It's soothing in a way I'm unfamiliar with. It brings the kind of peace I haven't felt since Daros escaped. I need Nash with me. Need his strength.

The knock sounds again, and I groan. Nash gets the tray. When he turns around, he grins.

My heart flutters.

"Should we eat?" he asks.

"Only if the food isn't poisoned." I laugh.

He makes to take a bite. I jump from my seat and whisk the piece of chicken from his fork with my bare hand. I take a small bite before he can stop me. "It's good," I say, not detecting anything.

He gives me a look. "You shouldn't have done that."

I suppose it wasn't very queenly of me. I shrug, put the chicken back on the plate and return to my seat.

He settles in next to me, and we eat our food in silence, though with many stolen glances. It's a nice sort of silence, the kind that is calming and perfect.

Once lunch is over, I put my plate on the low table nearby. "There is something you can do for me."

"What's that?" He puts his plate away.

"We should fight." I stand, kicking off my heels.

"On a full stomach?"

"You have to be ready to train at any time." It would be nice if we could ask for a training room, but seeing how we're not supposed to touch and we do that a lot when we fight, I don't trust that no one would see us.

He shakes his head with a laugh. "Honestly, I'm not sure I'm ready to be beaten by you again."

"Then don't let me get my hands around your throat."

He sighs. "At least you took your shoes off this time."

Together, we push the table back. The rest of the furniture is out of the way. I don't give him any warning. I dive for his thigh. Before I can get there, he jumps out of the way and brings a knee up to my hands.

I bounce back, startled. "No one's ever pulled that move on me before."

"I didn't think it would work."

"It won't, next time."

He laughs.

When I come at him, I don't stop when he backs up against a chair. I swerve to the side, jump up on the chair, grab his shoulder to keep him in place, and hop on his back. I wrap my legs around his waist as he attempts to pry me off.

I shiver from touching him. I wouldn't want it any other way, so I cling to him as hard as I can and enjoy the feel of his back against me.

He drops to the floor and rolls over, sending me gasping for air. When he rolls again, I don't have enough strength to hang on. I curse myself for getting lost in the feel of him, distracting me from my original intent.

I attempt to sit up, but he pins me to the ground. I grin, loving the warmth between us. "Very well done."

"You're going easy on me."

Maybe, but not for the reasons he believes. I'm not sure I even understand the reasons fully.

When neither of us moves, he says, "You give in?"

I giggle and squirm. "Not happening."

I go limp, and the pressure from him eases a little. I take advantage of the moment to slip out from under his arms, brushing my hand against his bicep as I climb on his back again.

He grunts. "I should have known better."

"Yes, you should have." I squeeze myself onto him, not letting anything get past. Nothing will distract me this time. Even if he does smell good.

I lock my arms around his throat, remembering the first time we fought together. It sends waves of thrills through me. What I wouldn't give to stay like this for a long, long time. Well, maybe not on his back, but with him.

"You should never let an opponent get on your back like this," I say.

"You're telling me," he gasps out.

He falls to the ground again, trying to roll over like he did the first time. I cling to him. When I don't fall off, he rolls a few more times until we're at the edge of the room, near some chairs. I breathe in deeply, letting his scent fill me, even as I tighten my grip.

"How do you always stick to me like this?" he gasps out again.

Because I never want to let him go. I don't say it aloud, though. I don't dare. It's not worth jinxing. Or worse, being rejected.

He pounds the ground three times, and I let go. "You give up?" I ask.

He catches his breath. "How can I not? It's either give up or pass out."

I look him square in the eye, ignoring the pounding in my heart. "Never give up."

"I won't." His words come out a whisper, and I know he's not talking about the fight.

We climb to our feet. He stretches.

"You fight well," I say.

"I lost."

"You fight well anyway."

We stare at each other. His hazel eyes have a sparkle to them that wasn't there before. I take a step forward.

"I should go," he says.

"Oh." I step back. "Right."

He turns around when he reaches the door. He opens his mouth. Closes it. Opens it again.

"Just say it." I'm eager for his words, whatever they may be.

"I had fun with you." He hurries from the room, with me grinning at his back.

CHAPTER 6

THE CITY LIES before me in a glorious array of flickering lights. My city. My people. My country.

Sometimes it's easy to forget about the people outside Indell. I've been to other cities in Valcora, but most of my assassin work was done in Indell. It's such a huge, sprawling place, but there are other cities out there too. Other people that need more help than lower taxes.

I watch the soldiers on the wall surrounding the palace. They all do their jobs, paying strict attention to the outside of the walls away from the palace. They keep us safe.

A guard turns around, the torchlight from below casting an eerie glow on him.

Daros.

I shrink back into the shadows, willing myself to become invisible. My heart gallops, knife blades cutting into my gut. When I look again, the guard looks nothing like Daros. He calls to a man below him on the grass. The two converse for a moment, and then the guard turns back to his job. I can't believe I thought it was Daros.

But he's out there.

I have to get my mind off him and do something more useful. I walk farther from my room more toward the center of the building, but the memories are still flooding me.

He had me by the throat—choked me for not coming down to his office directly when he asked me to. I sputtered for air, willing it all to end one way or another.

He pulled out his jeweled dagger, the one with precious gems along the hilt. He caressed my cheek with the blade, the cool metal biting into me without cutting. He did the same to the other cheek, and then shoved me away with a laugh. I stumbled to the floor.

When I glanced up, all I saw was that dagger. What would he do to me next?

A cool breeze whips across my skin. I pull myself from the memory, quivering. There's no point in reliving those moments when they haunt my subconscious all the time.

I wander around the roof, getting my bearings of this part of the palace. More like giving my mind a task to focus on. Once I have a better handle on things, I shimmy back down to my room. There is still a lot to explore, but there are always other nights.

I change into some nightwear and climb onto the bed that always leaves me feeling spoiled. It's much too nice for someone like me, but here I am, anyway.

It doesn't take long to fall asleep.

The First Queen is waiting for me. "You lowered taxes for some and raised them for others."

"Was that the wrong choice to make? What do you think?" I bite my lower lip. I'm more relaxed around her than when she started visiting my dreams.

"I think the Poruah and Medi will appreciate what you're doing for them."

"And the Kurah?" Not that I expect them to be happy, but it'd be nice if they were content.

"Time will tell."

"That's not helpful."

She sits there, serene as ever.

"Why do I dream of you, if this is all the help you're going to give me?" I plop back into a seat that isn't there.

"I want you to learn for yourself. I'm here to guide you."

"Is that why the last queen, Deedra, raised taxes? Because you only guided her?"

"Deedra was different than you. She needed different things. You're the most straightforward queen this country has ever seen."

I'm straightforward?

She chuckles. "Very much so."

Funny, since I'm used to evading everything.

"Yes, it is. You hide what you want well, but you don't always wish to."

No. I didn't. "Tell me something I should know about changing laws."

"You're changing the subject," she says, but lets it go. "You're going to have to deal with the council. They don't approve the laws—only you do that—but they'll be put out that you didn't consult them before making this change."

"They will be, won't they?" I sigh. I remember being on the roof. Of thinking I saw Daros.

"Your thoughts are straying to him again. Why do you let him hold so much power over you?"

"You can dive into my memories. You tell me." It's hard not to be annoyed.

"Not those memories. They are like a fortress against me."

Thank my daggers. It's hard enough, dealing with them, without talking to her about them.

"You really should talk to someone about those times. You'll feel better."

I don't respond.

"As queen, you have to be better. You're above everyone else. You need to let go of your feelings about Daros. About killing the last queen."

There's a prickling behind my eyelids. "It's not something you get over. I killed her. I killed many."

"I know, but it wasn't your choice. It was Daros's. He had you trained so you would do anything he told you to."

Maybe. Maybe not.

"No maybe." *Her voice is stern. "You had very little say in the things he had you do."*

Until I killed Deedra and couldn't live with myself anymore. I don't want to think about it, let alone talk about it. There is something, though. "If you are with all the queens, how come you didn't know I was the one who killed her? She saw me before I..." Stabbed her.

"You were in disguise."

"But you didn't recognize anything about me?"

She studies me. "I should have recognized your eyes. But before, no. I thought any familiarity was due to your drinking the Mortum Tura, since you now had part of me running through you."

It's so strange that she is a part of me now.

"It used to be strange for me too, but no longer." She shrugs.

"You've been guiding queens for how long?"

She smiles. "It's time to wake up."

CHAPTER 7

I SIT ON MY CHAIR, and the council follows suit. Nash's presence next to me is warming. Feeling him near reminds me of the hug he gave me. The kiss we shared.

I want more of that.

"Queen Ryn has called us all together to discuss the new tax laws," Nash says.

The council focuses on me. I wish there was a window in this room. All I get is pictures of Valcora.

"What I would like to know is why you did it without consulting us first," Timit, the Head of Treasury, says. His chins are a sign of wealth and prestige, but all I see is a man who wants to get his way.

The First Queen was right. I should have spoken to them about it. I just wanted to make it happen. Of course the Head of Treasury is not going to be happy with my choice. He never seemed to like me before, and his scowl indicates it's worse now than ever.

"Because," I say, "I'm ready to make that change for the people. I felt that telling them would be the best thing to do, to give them hope. To have them feel better. I'd like you to oversee the tax changes, Timit, and report back to me directly."

He puckers his lips like he ate something sour. "Yes, Your Majesty."

"I, for one, would like to commend you," Yuka says. Her sleek black hair is pulled away from her face. "Though it's customary to speak with the council first, you didn't have to, and you made a lot of people very happy."

I give her a soft smile but don't go so far as to thank her in front of everyone.

"It was a stupid move," Kada, Head of Relations, says. "How are we going to continue funding everything, the necessities? Even with raising taxes on the rich, it's not going to be enough."

I shrug trying to ignore the sting of her words. Daros was harsher, but being queen, I'd think they'd treat me better. "We'll use less."

"Less?" Timit practically screeches.

"It won't be hard to do. For starters, we can close down parts of the palace. It's much too big to utilize in its entirety."

"That would be a wise move," Mina, Head of Foreign Relations, says. Her fringe of red hair makes her stand out.

Now I have two people on my side. I smile at her as well.

"Fine," Timit says. "We'll use less of the palace, but anything else is not to be stood for."

Fickle man. "We'll do what we need to. If you don't like it, you're welcome to continue voicing your opinion or even leave, if you can't help it."

He clenches his jaw but says nothing further.

"Are there any other objections?" I ask.

"I'm not necessarily for it or against it," Jaku says, "but I would like to know how we're going to continue to pay for the men who guard you and the palace, and those who keep the peace across the country."

Good thought, though we did raise taxes to cover such a thing,

I need to be certain. "Is there not enough to cover that with the new changes?" I focus on Timit.

"I will have to look into it."

"You can report that back to me soon. We have to keep the basic needs of the government running—the guard, the military... We have mines of gold and precious gems. Where is all that wealth going?" The people—they need protection. I won't have them going without. "I'm sure we can make adjustments, to keep things going as they should."

"And what about the arts?" Yuka says. "I am for the changes, but we want to keep our culture."

"And food, of course. We have to continue to produce or purchase enough for everyone in the government. Can't do that without money." Nidon, the Head of Food, has a weight greater than Timit's somehow. I'll never be lucky enough to be like that even though I'm Queen now. I spend too much time exercising to gain that status.

"We will make sure everyone is taken care of." Though I'm not sure how. "We'll make sacrifices, but we can't ask our people to make those sacrifices on our behalf. They're suffering too much. We need this country to flourish, not drown in misery."

For once, they're quiet.

"Thank you for coming," I say.

I stand, and they all jump to their feet, though some not as fast as others. Nash and my escorts follow me out.

As we walk through the halls, back toward my rooms, Nash says, "That went well."

"You think so?"

"I do. You have a knack for caring about what's important."

Funny, since I spent so many years not caring. I thought it was tortured out of me. Maybe there's hope for me.

CHAPTER 8

IT'S BEEN several days since the council meeting, and I haven't heard back from Timit. It'd better not be because he's finding problems with the tax changes.

My ladies-in-waiting are gathered in my sitting room. Jem has taken the far chair again, with Inyi next to her. The rest are spread out in different seats than before. It makes it harder to remember their names, but I try. I've been practicing in my free time.

I get right to business. "How are the people handling the change in taxes?"

Jem surprises me by looking thoughtful instead of irritated. She surprises me more by answering. "The people I visited with were the lowest class. They have nothing but good things to say about you."

I'm shocked she went to speak to the lower class. But how much do I know about Jem, anyway? Only that she's been hostile to me since I arrived. That Borkus, Ranen, and Faya thought they could control her as the queen. That she tried to help me, though it seemed begrudging. Until now.

"What sorts of things are they saying about the taxes?" I ask.

"That you are meant to be queen, with what you've done." Her eyebrows are drawn together.

Hmm. "What about others? Did anyone else visit the Poruah?"

"I went with Jem, Your Majesty," Inyi says.

Not surprising.

"The people were as Jem said," she continues. "Their praise toward you was extraordinary."

I shift. Not what I was going for. I just want to ease their burdens, so they can buy food. Clothes. Shelter. Things that have been hard for them to obtain.

"I also went to the Poruah," Lipla says. "They were rather greedy, Your Highness."

This puzzles me. "In what way?"

"They wanted all that tax money and to surround themselves with things they don't need, and they are taking advantage of you to do it."

I press my lips together. It's better I don't respond to that. Wanting necessities or even the occasional luxury is not taking advantage of me. Then again, without seeing it for myself, who am I to know what they really do want or not?

"I went to many of the Medi, Your Majesty." Freza is closest to me on the left. The spot of honor, though she placed herself there.

I wonder if that means anything. "What did they have to say?"

"They think you're brilliant, as well. They can now afford to continue on as Medi and not fall to Poruah, at least the ones I talked to."

"Those I spoke with as well," Pina, the youngest, adds. "They were all very pleased, Your Majesty."

Hmm. "And the Kurah?"

"Forgive me, Your Majesty," Suyla says. "They aren't pleased. They feel it's unfair for them to take the brunt of the taxes."

Maybe it is, but they can afford the most without their quality of life taking a hit. "And what does everyone here think? Do you think it's unfair for me to tax the rich?"

There's a lot of fidgeting and avoiding eye contact.

Finally, Jem says, "I think it's hard to say what's fair."

This surprises me. Not the words, but that they're coming from her. Maybe she has more to offer than I first thought? "What do you mean?"

"What may be fair to one person may be unfair to another. It's hard to judge for an entire people what's fair when it varies from person to person."

"What else do you ladies think?" I ask.

"You should change things back to how they were," Lipla says. "This won't benefit the crown in any way."

"What if I'm not trying to benefit the crown? What if I'm trying to benefit the people?"

She narrows her eyes before she looks to the floor. The skin around her mouth is tense. She's not happy with my answer.

"It's a nice aspiration, Your Highness, but I'm not sure it's realistic." Benala is the oldest left of my ladies-in-waiting, in her forties. She has bright-blue eyes, brown hair, and a usually happy countenance that's subdued today.

"Why is that?" I ask.

"Because the Kurah are sure to rebel. They aren't going to stand for having higher taxes. The Poruah and Medi need to do their part as well."

"I'm not saying they shouldn't, but their share wasn't fair in this."

"Who are you to decide what's fair?"

I'm surprised the question comes from Lipla, not Jem. I give her a piercing gaze. "I am the queen."

"Rightly so, Your Majesty." Jem's voice isn't as hostile as I'm used to. I don't know what to make of it. "But I think, given that you didn't train with us, there is the question of whether you should have sought our council before making such a decision."

Not hostile, but not on my side either.

I don't trust her change. I plan on keeping her close, so I can pay attention to her. I don't want another Faya.

"I've lived among the people." For a short time anyway. "I've seen their struggles. Seen what the lack of essentials looks like. Everyone has a right to life. To more than only starving on the streets." That quiets them, but there's more I need to know. "How's productivity?"

"The work load is up," Pina says. "The people are happier and buying more at the market. Not just food, either. I think this is a real success, Your Majesty."

This coming from the youngest. I'm not sure what to think. Except that it's time for another outing.

CHAPTER 9

Iᴛ's hard to talk Nash into going out again. He thinks my safety is paramount. While it is important, there are some things I need to see for myself. Luckily, I'm able to talk him into going in disguise and with a couple of guards, like I did once before.

The market is full of the scents of fresh bread and roasted duck. I inhale, grateful I was smart enough to bring money this time. I have to be cautious with it, since it's the people's money. What better use for it than to give it back to them, though?

I buy Nash and me some meat on a stick. He shakes his head but has no problem digging in.

"You like it?" I ask.

"It's excellent."

"Good." Once we finish this succulent treat, we wander through the market. It's much different than before. People are buying things, smiling, and chatting with one another, in a manner that exudes happiness. I turn to Nash. "What do you think about what you see?"

"It looks like the people are doing much better than last time we were here."

"I think so too."

We continue our stroll, taking everything in. I spot a girl that looks familiar. I try to place her, but all that comes to mind is being alone in the dark. I know who she is—the girl I traded clothes with after leaving Daros's for the first time. She's still wearing what I gave her, though dirtier and more tattered.

"Come over here," I ask of Nash and lead him to the girl.

She looks at us quizzically. "Can I help you?"

"No, but you did, once." I pull out a handful of coins. "I want you to have this."

She widens her eyes. "I can't accept such a gift."

"Please take it. It's yours. You assisted me in a time I really needed it. This is the least I can do, to repay you."

Slowly, she holds out her hand, and I drop the coins inside. I hurry off before she can change her mind.

"What was that about?" Nash asks.

"She gave me clothes when I escaped Daros's. She offered to help me. Let me stay with her family. Although I didn't, I haven't forgotten her kindness."

We come to a corner that has a man plucking out a tune on a vilka, a stringed instrument. A couple starts dancing to the music, stepping high and clapping their hands. Another couple joins. And another.

"Let's go." I want to pull Nash toward the dancing group but hope my words are enough.

"I'm not sure we should."

"Come on. It'll be fun." I glance around and find Wilric, Afet, and Eldim surrounding us at different parts.

I stand next to a woman, lift my feet to the music and pound them against the cobblestone. I clap my hands in time with the rhythm. It's a bouncy, happy song. The dance doesn't seem to have specific steps, just a twirling, dipping, flying into the air, and spinning around to the beat.

Dancing across from me, Nash's lips twitch. Then turn up.

Then become a full-fledged grin. He's enjoying this as much as I am.

The others start kicking their feet up high. Nash and I follow suit. It's a good workout. If I didn't exercise every day, I'd be out of breath. The women twirl in place. I do the same, laughing as the world spins around me.

Then I see him.

Daros.

I fall to the ground, pulling out a dagger as I go.

The lady next to me bends down to help me, but shies away when she sees what I'm holding.

Nash is at my side in an instant. "Are you all right? That looked like it hurt."

"Daros," is all I can get out.

As I stand, Nash draws a dagger of his own. The people give us a wide berth as my guards close in around us.

A faint breeze of whispers quickly turn into a full-blown wind. I don't care; I must find him.

I scan the area, but there's no one who looks a thing like him—bulky, yet muscled, with short brown hair and thick eyebrows.

"I don't see him anymore." My chest is constricted. Tight. Unwavering.

"It's all right," Nash says, as we move away from where I saw Daros. "Take a deep breath."

I gasp for air that doesn't want to make its way past my throat. I look around in a frenzied motion.

"I'm right here." Nash uses a soft voice but loud enough it reaches me. "I won't let him hurt you."

No one can promise that.

Not even Nash.

Wilric reaches us first. "What happened?"

"She spotted Daros."

Wilric pulls out his sword without hesitation, and the others do the same, though they haven't gotten to us yet. They check the crowd like I am doing.

The group gathered around us gives us more space, watching us with big eyes. Except for one man, who doesn't look familiar but is staring at me as if he knows me. Out of nowhere, he calls out, "It's the queen."

A gasp goes through the crowd.

Anger at Daros distracts me. Makes it hard to think. Do I deny who I am? Admit it? Ignore them and run? Everyone is staring at me. I try to neutralize my expression. When that doesn't work, I fill it with something besides anger.

"She's not in the palace?" a man asks.

"Have you come to offer us more good news?" a female calls out.

"Praise the queen," another female yells. "All praise the queen."

Then one person starts to clap, and soon, more join. A cry of joy goes up, as the clapping grows. Soon it's a dull roar, pounding in my ears.

If I wasn't so filled with fury, I'd be embarrassed.

Or filled with awe.

These people are cheering for me. For what I've done. I can't believe it.

My breathing calms, and my senses come back to me. I smile at the people as I scan the crowd for him. They wave, and I wave back, sending squeals throughout the crowd. They press forward, and my heart drops. This is how Daros could get close to me. Through the people wanting to be near me.

A guard with her sword out calls out, "Back up. Give the queen some space."

They stop closing in, but the cheering continues.

"We've got to get the queen back to the palace," Wilric says over the noise.

Afet leads the way saying, "Make way for the queen."

Soon a path opens up behind Afet. Wilric motions me forward.

Nash hurries to my side, pulling out his sword to go with his dagger. Eldim stays close behind us.

As I hurry through the way Afet has opened up, the people call out more things while closing the way behind us.

"Bless you, Your Majesty."

"You've brought us peace."

"Thank you for giving us means to buy food."

"You are our savior."

The words blur together. One thing is clear—the people that frequent this market love what I have done for them. No doubt the upper class isn't as happy.

But right here, right now, I feel the power of the people enough that I'm less worried about Daros. If he tried to attack me in this frenzy, he'd have more than my guards to contend with.

At least I'd like to think my people are not cowards. Not when they voice their opinions so freely.

As we hurry away from the market, the crowd follows us, cheering and calling out words of praise. More join, making the group grow to epic proportions. By the time we get to the grass strips by the wall surrounding the palace, the voices of the crowd are deafening.

Other guards help us as they see our plight. Not that we're being threatened by the crowd; they're being magnificently respectful. Still, they are many, and somewhere in among them, Daros is waiting for me.

The guards surround us and usher us through the portcullis. I get closer to the palace while the people stay on the other side of the wall, but the cheering can be heard.

Jaku appears at my side. "What happened, Your Majesty?"

I glance at Nash. I don't have to explain; I am their leader. I find myself doing so, anyway. "I was in disguise, but the people recognized me."

"Not only that," Nash says. "She also spotted Daros in the market."

"I'll get men out in the market right now, to search for him." Jaku yells orders to the men behind me.

My personal escorts and Nash hurry me in the building and through the halls. As soon as we get in my rooms, Nash lets out a sigh. "That did not go as I planned."

"So much for my guise."

"I'll say. No more going out in public without a retinue and a plan. Maybe not at all, until we catch Daros."

As much as I agree with him, it's a sobering thought. The people were so excited to see me. I want to be out among them more. Is there something I can do to help them without risking my safety?

I must find out.

CHAPTER 10

TONIGHT, there's no meeting with the First Queen. No nightmares either, so I can't complain. Still, I miss talking with her. I want to share my excitement over what happened with the people.

I'm refreshed from yesterday. Something about the people's enthusiasm was draining. Not to mention the fear and anger toward Daros.

Was that really him in the market yesterday? Jaku's men never found any sign of him, though it would be easy for him to get lost in such a large crowd. If it was him, how did he know where to find me? Or did he stumble onto me? I didn't even know I was going to be going out yesterday. Unless one of my closest guards told someone, passed a message in the market when no one was looking, or something along those lines, how could Daros have found me?

I don't want to believe I was betrayed, but I can't eliminate it either until I know what happened. Then again, I may never know.

The thought is depressing.

"Good morning, Your Majesty." Inkga comes in with our breakfast trays.

I insist on us eating together every morning. The danger of poisoning seems to have passed and others taste the food before it gets to us, yet I still scout out our food before we eat it. Besides, eating in front of her was strange. Like when Daros forced me to go without. I can't handle being like him.

"Morning." I check both plates for signs of poison. When I find none, I grin. "Looks good this morning."

Ham, eggs, pastries, and fruit fill our trays. Knowing my people will be having something for breakfast as well makes it more appetizing.

"You're sure digging in with zeal this morning." She takes a dainty bite of pastry.

"Hungry."

She laughs.

Once I've gotten a better handle on my hunger, I ask, "What do you think of Jem?"

She freezes with the fork halfway to her mouth. It takes her a moment, but she brings it to her mouth, chews, and swallows. "She's much different than you. Why do you ask?"

"I'm trying to get a feel for her. She's hard to read."

"She does tend to keep to herself, but I suppose that's normal behavior toward me—a servant. Only you don't seem to mind my station."

"No reason to." Maybe Jem is conceited?

"You have to understand that Jem grew up knowing she might become queen one day. She's trained her whole life to act a certain way, either as a queen or a lady-in-waiting. There's not much you could do to change that,."

"Do you think that's the reason she is the way she is?"

"At least partly. I don't know her that well, though." After several minutes of silence, she asks, "How was your outing yesterday?"

"Have you heard much about it?"

"Just that you gathered a crowd."

Possibly including Daros, and I didn't catch him. I hold back a shudder. I need him found. Need him dealt with. As for the crowd... "It was a different experience. I've had them all bow to me before, but this adoring. I don't know what to do with that sort of attitude toward me."

"It would be a difficult thing to deal with."

"I confess I don't know how to handle it—what I should do with their attentions."

"I'm sure it will come with practice."

"Do you believe so?"

"I do."

After we finish eating, I dress while she clears the plates. It's a simple outfit—a black skirt with holes in the pockets for my daggers and a cream top. She helps me with my hair before excusing herself. I won't see her again until tonight unless I call for her.

I wait in my sitting room for my ladies-in-waiting. They don't take long to arrive.

"How are you all this morning?" I ask.

I get mixed answers, from *well* to *wonderful*. No one claims to be ill or sad. They never do.

I want to change their unwillingness to speak discomforts as well one day.

"What should we discuss today?" I ask.

"We didn't realize you were going out yesterday," Inyi says. "I would have dearly loved to go with you, Your Majesty."

"I didn't know you would want to."

"Oh yes. I would."

"As would I," Pina says.

Others chime in that they'd like to be included.

Something to think about. "I'm sorry to say we won't be going out for a while. While I was out there, I thought maybe I should meet with the people more often, but I can't be in public right now. Any suggestions on meeting with them more often? What should I do?"

"Why can't you leave the palace, Your Highness?" Lipla asks.

Freza elbows her in a not-so-subtle way.

"It's all right," I reply, though they've probably heard the gossip. "Almost everyone knows Daros escaped the dungeons. It's not safe on the streets."

"For you, or for anyone?" Pina's face is tight.

Good question. "I'm not sure what he has planned, so it's hard to say. Any other thoughts on how to connect with the people?"

"I have one." Jem's voice rings out with authority. She might have made a better queen than me. "Why don't you meet with your subjects in the throne room?" She's not sarcastic, but sounds like she doesn't believe I'll take her up on the offer.

"Maybe." It's worth thinking about at least. It would include less exposure for me. It's something I should have thought about before, but without proper training and not dealing with the previous queens, it never crossed my mind to do it that way.

"You could have Jaku set up guards, to search everyone who comes through, and limit how many you see at a time, like you did at the ball." If I didn't know better, I'd say she almost sounds excited.

"It's not half bad. What do the rest of you think?" I can't believe I'm taking ideas from Jem. She did do a good job, helping with the ball, though, and now she has a good plan. I shouldn't shun her just because our personalities are incompatible.

"Would you accept anyone who wished to see you?" Lipla asks.

I shrug. "As long as they aren't a criminal and don't have a weapon on them, I don't see what it would hurt."

She presses her lips together. "Even the Poruah?"

"Especially them." I give her a big smile, though it feels forced.

"I don't think a queen should stoop to mingling with those of the lower class." She sniffs, head held high.

"Think about it this way," Jem says to her, startling me with her frustration turned to someone besides me. "The Poruah are the ones our economy is built on. The majority of our people fall into that class. By helping them, we help our entire nation."

I stare at her. I hadn't thought of it like this. I wanted to tend to everyone, but I didn't realize there were so many Poruah. What's more, I didn't realize Jem cared about them. Maybe she is more concerned about the country than I first suspected.

I doubt Faya and Ranen would have been able to control her like they thought they would.

"Thank you for putting it so well, Jem," I say.

It's her turn to look at me with eyes widened enough that I can tell she's shocked. She says nothing further, just gives me a slight nod.

"Does anyone have anything to add?" When no one answers, I say, "Good. I have a meeting with the council. Please let me know if something comes up before we meet again. I'll be thinking about what you said today." I glance at Jem, but she's looking at her hands.

They stand, give me their goodbyes with their curtseys, and are gone.

Nash comes in as they leave. "Are you ready for another meeting?" He moves closer to me.

I stand so we can be as near as possible without actually touching. His warmth is soothing. Makes me forget myself.

It's dangerous, but in a most delicious way.

"I am." I brush my skirt down. I miss wearing pants, like I often do.

"Before we go, I just wanted to tell you I'm glad everything turned out all right yesterday and you're safe. And I'm sorry we haven't caught Daros yet. I can't imagine how much that must bother you."

I clear my throat. "Yes, well... I'm disappointed they didn't find him, but I didn't expect them to. It would have happened if Daros wanted it to."

He reaches out to touch me, but pulls away at the last minute.

"Don't do that," I say.

"Don't do what?"

I give him a look.

He runs his hands through his hair. "I'm sorry. I know you're all right with touching, but it's against the law. I could be put to death for it if we got caught."

It's extreme for them to kill him just for touching me. It's not like I can get pregnant from a single touch, but then, maybe they're trying to prevent escalating to that by being so extreme. "I'm the queen. Can't I control the laws?"

"Not this one. It's been a law as long as anyone can remember. The unbreakable law. It's there to protect our country, not give into the whims of a queen's desires is what they say. It can't be changed."

I scowl. "It should be."

"I don't know. As much as I want it to be allowed, for us to be able to touch each other, I don't want our country to fall into chaos again, like it did years ago when they tried changing things."

He means the time when our people were almost destroyed by natural disasters, one hundred and fifty years ago. "Do you believe the nation was hit by tempests, earthquakes, and plagues because someone tried to change things?"

"I don't know, but it's not something I want to take a chance on."

I sigh. "You're right. I just…" I hesitate before ghosting my fingertips over his. I want more. I want to actually touch him. To get that hug he gave me the other day. That kiss against my lips.

"I do too." His voice is soft.

I step back, before I do something we'll both regret. "We should get going to the council meeting."

"Right. They're probably waiting for you." He moves away from me.

"Thank you for being so patient with me."

He turns and winks. "That's what Head Advisors are for."

Together with my escorts, we go down to the council room. It seems like more and more occasions are spent here. I'm getting rather tired of it. It's about time for another walk in the garden afterward. Too bad I don't have time.

CHAPTER 11

THE COUNCIL MEETING IS QUICK, though not quick enough for my tastes. Will I ever get used to this? Talking about little details of government that others consider important, like what party we need to throw next or who to invite, I could do without. Some things I know are crucial, such as hearing updates on the people and how the guard's training is going. Even then, I can only listen to so much of it, and I'm afraid I tuned most of it out. I need to get better at this, which might happen with time. I know I can if I set my mind to it.

The halls of the palace are clear of anyone except Nash, my escorts, and me. The steady sound of our footsteps echo, bringing some life with them. It would be nice if we could pass a window where I might look out over the guard, but that's on the other side anyway.

As we head deeper in the building toward the dungeon to take care of something I should have a long time ago, I think about replacing my lost council member, Borkus. Head of Design isn't a position I feel I need to fill, but the council is asking for it. If only he hadn't been disloyal.

I sigh.

"Everything all right?" Nash asks.

I grin at him. "Dandy."

Unless you count what I'm about to do. Interviewing prisoners is not my favorite thing. It reminds me too much of what Daros did to me. I have to, though. Have to see if they're ready to give me any answers. None have been forthcoming to my guard, but maybe a personal touch is needed.

I trudge down the steps, not caring if my dress drags behind me. Despite where we are, the place is kept clean and well-lit by many torches, casting flickering lights across the brick walls. Not a spec of dirt on the floors or cobwebs on the walls.

The jailers get to their feet and bow. One of them, a woman with a rich voice and sharp features says, "Your Majesty, the prisoners are ready for you."

"Thank you."

Nash leads the way to Borkus's cell. When we get there, Wilric hits the bars with the hilt of his sword. "Borkus, you have a visitor."

Borkus rolls over on his bed, turning his back to us. There's not much in his room—a bucket in the corner and a bed that's probably softer than he deserves.

I've been in worse places.

"Tell me why you wanted Jem on the throne," I say.

There's no response.

"The queen asked you a question." Nash is tense by my side, his hands on his hips.

Borkus rolls over and lowers his feet to the floor. He doesn't look up. "If you want answers, you should be asking Ranen. He was the one behind this."

This is more of an answer than I've ever gotten. I wonder if being locked up is getting to him.

"Why did you go along with it?" I ask.

"Because Ranen promised me I could assist with the government's fashion. That I would be the leader of fashion. That he'd help increase my popularity with the Kurah, so they would come to me for their needs." His voice is weary.

A lot more reasons I thought, some better than others. "And you thought that was worth my life?"

He slouches his shoulders more than they already were.

I wait, but he says nothing further.

I nod for Nash to take me to Ranen. He's several cells over, far enough it would be hard for him to hear what Borkus said so the two of them can't conspire. He's also nowhere near those he hired to bring me to my death. I'm not sure what to do with them all. I don't want to kill them, but I hate leaving them here, when at any moment they could escape like Daros. Though there are less ways to do so now that we've upped security, but the thoughts still creep in.

I'm grateful Daros didn't take any of them with him.

Thinking of Daros while down here is the wrong thing to do. I shiver.

Nash pulls off his coat and hands it to me.

"Thank you." I'm careful to not touch his hand as I take it and wrap it around my shoulders.

I wasn't cold, but his coat is warm with him. The exact comfort I need.

When we reach Ranen's cell, he's standing against the bars like he was waiting for us. I've interviewed him before, but at random times, though you lose track of time in situations like this.

I always did.

"Look who's come for a visit." Without his tasseled hat, Ranen is bald. He's thinner than he used to be too, though not because we don't feed him. His dark gaze takes in everything about me, lingering on Nash's coat.

"I want to know why you thought you could control Jem if she was on the throne." I sound firm. In control. Good.

"Are you missing someone? Another prisoner perhaps?" he asks.

A chill sweeps through me, but I keep my voice steady. "I don't know what you're talking about."

"Oh, come on now. People talk, even down here, no matter how hard you try to prevent it." He sounds as haughty as always.

It takes a lot of willpower not to clench my jaw, pinch my fingers together, or show him any other sign of being upset. "Tell me about Jem."

"You won't get what you want from me. Not now, not ever."

There are many things I could threaten him with. Take away his food. His bed. His water. Torture him within a breath of his life.

I won't.

I'm stronger than that.

But—oh—how I want to. "Why did you think you could control Jem?" I want to know if I can trust her or not, but I should have known I wouldn't get an answer from him.

Ranen narrows his dark eyes at me. Suddenly, he pushes against the bars with such force that I jump back. He laughs like he isn't the one trapped in this dungeon.

I give him one final glance before turning back toward the entrance. I won't bother with him again for a while. I'll have to judge Jem for myself.

When we get to my sitting room, I invite Nash in. It's almost dinner time, and I have a meal planned with the council and some of the upper class that's sure to be a doozy.

"Did you need something?" Nash asks.

I take his coat off and hand it back to him, though I have the desire to keep it and sleep in it. Wear it whenever I need his comfort but can't have it. But there's no way I can.

"I don't know what I need." My answer surprises me.

"I wish I could help you. Give you whatever it is you do need." He sounds so sincere. It makes my eyes prickle.

"You give me more than anyone else. You give me everything." It's not something I should say.

I glance up at him through my lashes, grateful we're alone. That I can smell the scent of him—metal and earth. See into his hazel and blue eyes. He's captivating and watching me as closely as I'm looking at him.

"I don't give you nearly enough." His voice is a whisper across my skin. "Tell me what's bothering you. Open up to me. Let me help."

Can I? It's not something I like to do; people betray you when you open up to them. But this is Nash. He's proven himself to me time and time again. I don't think he'll betray me. But that's the problem.

Think.

It's such a little word, but one that makes me hesitate. I can face fighting men twice my size, but I can't stand putting myself out there. This is silly. I can be brave enough. It's Nash.

When the words come, they're small. "I'm scared."

His arms are around me, pulling me close. I rest my head against his shoulder and place a hand on his chest. His comfort envelops me. Makes me want to be with him more. Makes me want to give him everything I can.

"Tell me about it." His voice is soft but firm. Reassuring.

"It's Daros. He's after me—I know it. I worry for me, for you... for everyone around me. I don't know what he's going to do next. What's going to happen to me or those I care about. It feels dangerous. Precarious."

"I won't let anything bad happen to anyone."

I want to believe him. Ache to. Only— "No one can stop Daros when he puts his mind to something."

"You did once before. We can stop him again."

It's what the First Queen said, but can it be true? I don't know. It's hard to believe. Hard to follow.

He cups the back of my head. I close my eyes and ease into it. It's soothing. Calming.

But I have those fears biting away at me.

We pull apart enough that we can look into each other's eyes.

He says nothing more. He doesn't have to. It's in his eyes.

On his lips.

I lean in.

He moves closer.

I close my eyes.

His lips brush against mine. Soft at first—a feather against my skin—and then harder. Firmer. Stronger. Everything I want in him. In his kiss.

As the pressure on my lips increases, I wrap my arms around him and pull him closer. He threads his fingers through my hair, pushing me to him. I savor the taste of him. To enjoy the way he feels against me.

We should have kissed long ago.

There was no point waiting after our first kiss or of becoming cold with each other. We belong together. It is a fact I believe in more than anything else. This is true and right. The way his lips move beneath mine is like a shining beacon of hope into my soul.

We belong together.

We are together.

The kiss is perfect. Even better than the first one. It's soft and kind, yet hard and demanding. Everything I wanted without realizing I wanted it.

I don't know how much time passes before the kiss ends, but it doesn't feel like enough. We break away, and I'm breathless. By the way he's gasping for air, he feels the same. I don't know what got into us, but I want it to happen more often.

Except that it's against the law.

I'm not allowed to have relations.

It could get him killed.

I jerk away, unwilling to lose him just because of my desire. It's not what I want for him. For us. I want so much more than to see him ripped away from me.

But that kiss... Oh, that kiss...

I NEED IT AGAIN.

By the heat burning in his eyes, Nash needs it too.

His gaze molds across my lips, caressing my skin. I press my lips together, as if that will somehow fix what I can't have.

"We shouldn't have done that." Nash's words tear my heart into little pieces that are whisked away into the wind. "But I'm glad we did."

I close the distance between us, the guilt about touching him warring with my need for him and the desire to be comforted—to be healed by him.

"No one ever made me feel like this before." The words are out before I can stop them.

"I know what you mean."

"You do?"

He brushes a hair out of my eye and caresses my cheek with his thumb. "I do. I wouldn't change it for anything."

He caresses my cheek with his thumb. I lean into the touch, not wanting him to ever stop, but things will get in the way. "We have to be careful. I don't want anyone to hurt you."

"I know." He sighs as he moves away.

We're inches apart. Not far, yet we might as well be on opposite sides of the greatest chasm in the world.

"Your Head Advisor shouldn't act like this with you. No one should, according to the law, but especially me." My heart sinks at his words. "Yet I can't seem to help myself."

"You know this is good between us. We just have to be cautious, so no one finds out." But what about the First Queen? She's sure to know. What will she think of me? And what about my stained soul? Will it rub off on him? Affect him?

He takes a step back and rubs his shoulder. "We shouldn't do that anymore. But know that, if you ever need to talk about anything, I'm here. I will always be here."

My heart warms at the thought, even as it cringes.

Despite not being able to touch him—to kiss him—I am not alone.

CHAPTER 12

As the First Queen *comes into view, I can't help the stab of guilt that goes through me.*

"Do you want to discuss it?" *she asks.*

"Not really." *Except there is one thing.* "Why was that rule made, that no one can have relations with the queen?"

"I made it for the reasons you suspect."

"You were the one to put it into effect?"

"I did."

The two words hurt worse than I thought they would.

"I know it's not what you want, but it is dangerous for the queen to have relations."

"Didn't you say I should go for what I want?"

"You should, but only under the right circumstances, and I'm not sure these are the ones."

My heart sinks. "Are the stories true? Does the world turn to chaos when things change?"

"It does."

"Did you do that part?" *Because I don't like it. It's wrong.*

She hesitates. It makes me wish I could read her mind as well. "I did not."

"Who did?"

"Someone you'll never know."

"Because they're dead?"

"Yes. They've been gone for a long, long time."

It'd be nice if things were different, but it's not something I can change.

"Tell me about the people of the city," she says. "I know you visited with them. What did you think?"

I tell her all about them and find that the words flow. I am eager to talk about this. "I'm grateful they seem happy for the change, but I don't know how to respond to their attitude toward me. It's almost..."

"Worshipful." She fills in.

"Yes." My voice is hushed.

"You did something they appreciate. It's only natural that they turn around and praise you for it and show such adoration."

"But I gave them something they should have had anyway. They shouldn't be denied the basics of life."

"No. They shouldn't." The First Queen is very solemn.

After a moment, I ask, "What else do you think I should do for them? What has been done for them in the past?"

She cocks her head to the side. "A lot of things have been done for them that are good. One of the best policies was increased trade throughout the country. The people prospered during that period of time."

"Because they grew wealthier?" How else would it benefit them?

"That, and they also had more interactions with each other and grew happier. They liked getting to know one another. They opened their minds and came into contact with different viewpoints, developing their critical thinking."

What would it be like, to have the cities of my country more united? It sounds like a great plan, but hard to execute.

"It is hard," she says, "but if you put your mind to it, you could make it happen in a way that would have the people thriving."

It's what I desire for them. Why didn't the last queen do that?

"Because she didn't listen to my advice."

"Deedra seems like she wasn't the type of queen the country deserves."

"As you say."

Am I? I don't want to be the one who messes everything up for them.

"You are better for them than you know."

I open my eyes to morning, a bright, glorious new day. The First Queen's words still echo in my head. I hope she's right and that I'm better for them than I think.

CHAPTER 13

INKGA HELPS ME INTO A DRESS—A subdued thing in maroon, but stately, according to her. It has sleeves that blossom out at my elbows and reach the floor, where they meet my wide skirt. Wide for me. According to court trends, it's much too narrow.

She pins up my hair and places the silver headband on it, where the crown will go. The whole time I look over my shoulder, expecting to see Daros or one of his men.

They never show.

I insisted on only Inkga helping me prepare. I'm not certain I want to be around other people right now. Strange, since I'm about to be among hundreds, with all gazes trained on me.

The thought reminds me of when I first drank the Mortum Tura. Of having a death wish.

Now I long for life.

Enough so that I'm willing to fight Daros or anyone else who stands in my way. The change is welcome, but it feels as if the death wish is hovering just under the surface, ready to splash forth at any time.

I push those feelings aside. I'm better than this.

"There." Inkga puts the last touches on my short hair. "All finished. You look lovely."

"Thank you for making me so."

She beams at me like I gave her the best present. "You had it in you. I only spiffed it up a little."

A blush heats my cheeks.

There's a knock. I follow Inkga to the next room, and she answers it.

She says, "Your Head Advisor, Nash Zorris."

He strides in the room, and my breath falters. He looks good. Too good. His black boots come up to his knees. Cream pants, a black shirt, and a red overcoat with silver buttons complete his outfit. Though I don't like red, it looks good on him. The ring that belonged to his father is on his left hand ring finger. His brown hair is combed, and hazel eyes sparkle at me, though they are more subdued than usual.

I want to bring him closer, not push him away.

I want to embrace him.

Lose myself in his arms.

But I can't.

He gives a stiff bow. "Your Majesty. Everything is ready and waiting for you."

I nod, not trusting myself to speak to him. To Inkga, I say, "Thank you again, for all your help. Why don't you follow with the guards, so you can watch from a good spot? If you'd like."

"I would enjoy that. Thank you, Your Highness."

At least someone's happy with what's to come. Being queen is my duty now, but one I'm not certain I'm suited to.

I head out of the room, brushing past Nash without touching him. He's strong. Inviting. Entirely too so. I hurry on. Two of my escorts go in front of me, and everyone else follows behind. There's too much attention on me, and it's about to get worse.

We twist and turn through the hallways. I forget how big this building is when I stay in my own little area. It's silly that so many queens added to it over the years, making it a monstrosity. At least cleaning it keeps people having jobs.

When we finally reach the door to the throne room, more guards are waiting. One of them peeks inside. "They are ready for you, Your Majesty."

The guards go ahead and stand on the floor lower than me between the dais and the crowd. Nash, and Inkga shuffle in, where they hopefully can find seats close by. I should have asked Nash more about what to expect. I realize I'm pinching my fingers together, and I relax them.

I nod to the guard that I'm ready and enter the room to find it full to the brim with people.

My people.

They bow.

"Rise." My voice echoes through the room.

Like at the ball, there are people of all statuses here—from Kurah, in fine, overly ornate clothing; to the Medi, who are well dressed; to those Poruah in rags, who've made the effort to clean up. Eager eyes watch me as I move forward, focusing on the throne at the front of the room. It's too many steps away now to worry about, but I tread them anyway.

To the right of the throne is a table with a crown sitting on it. On the other side is another table, with the chalice that holds the Mortum Tura. I will drink it, like the First Queen recommended. It will make me more powerful, though I'm not exactly sure how.

It feels as if it takes a full minute to get to the throne, but it can't possibly be that long. I reach the throne, which behind it has guards by the wall facing the crowd. More guards stand in front of the people, Nash and Inkga next to them.

For one of the few times in my life, I want to smile at them, but I keep it tight inside. It's much too formal of an occasion for me to grin. I sit on the throne, feeling silly that I'm sitting while everyone else is on their feet. At least my back is no longer to the room, and I can see everything. Even Daros.

My heart stops.

I search the crowd with my gaze.

He's here to ruin everything, like he's always done before.

I can't find him again. Where is he? Nothing. No one familiar. Maybe my eyes played tricks on me. Maybe not. Either way, my jaw is clenched tight. I'm grateful for all the weapons stashed on my person. I'd be grateful for my guards too, but last time we were here, they were so stunned to find out I killed the last queen that they didn't help. I can't be sure they'll come to my aid in a fight.

"The Shadow Wraith can't be our queen." A richly dressed man runs up the aisle toward me, sword in hand.

A dagger is out before I can think, though I don't want to hurt one of my subjects. Before he gets close, several guards are pulling him out of the room.

He'll be taken to the dungeons, but hopefully not punished too harshly by the council. He may have tried to kill me, but I am the Shadow Wraith. I've left the country without many important men and women. He has reason to be upset with me, but that won't change me becoming queen.

I can't keep sitting here; the ceremony must go forward.

I put the dagger back, grasp the stem of the chalice, and bring it in front of me.

The room is hushed, gazes attentive.

This drink does more than make me queen. It has power within it. Makes me stronger. More powerful.

Is that what I want?

For my people's sake, yes.

I lift it to my lips and taste the Mortum Tura—pomegranate, flavored with chocolate. I finish the whole cup before setting it back down on the table, where it will refill itself.

There's a shiver. A rush of something twisting through me. It's like a pressure at the back of my head, but different. More.

A gasp goes through the crowd. I must be glowing, bright and strong—the true sign that I belong as queen.

I belong.

I pick up the crown. Lift it high above my head, stretching my arms. The gazes of those gathered prick through me.

There is no turning back, only moving forward.

I lower the crown onto my head.

It's heavier than I thought it would be, enough to weigh me down with the burden of caring for my people.

Those gathered fall to the floor, their foreheads touching the gleaming wood. Unlike the first time this happened, I know what to do, and I don't keep them waiting. "Please rise."

There's a rustle of movement as they climb back to their feet. So many people, all here for me, and this is just a small fraction.

Jaku comes forward, followed by the men under his command. He steps to the side, while the others come along the aisle I treaded across not that long ago, each stopping to bow to me and pledge their loyalty with a fist to their heart before I nod and they march back. I must nod over a thousand times.

The people must be restless—I know I am—but I appreciate the fact that the guards are promising themselves to protect and serve me.

Once the line ends, the guards protecting me each take a turn coming forward and doing the same, before lining back up where they were. They're doing their job—one they've done for about seven weeks now.

After they're all finished, Jaku comes forward. "Your Majesty, Queen Ryn. My men and I pledge our loyalty to you from now until the day my service is no longer needed. May your rule be long."

I nod at him like I did to the others, and he returns to his place among the council.

Nash comes forward then. My heart gives a light thump. He kneels before me, and I want to tell him to get up, but it's part of the ceremony. It's needed.

He puts his fist to his heart. "Queen Ryn, I pledge my loyalty to you from now until the day my services are no longer needed. May your rule be long."

I want to reach down. To touch him.

Instead, I nod.

He glances at me, and our gazes meet. For one moment, time is ours.

And then it's over.

He moves back to his spot behind the guards, and the next council member comes forward. They all do and say what Nash did, only none of them make me want to jump out of my throne and throw my arms around them.

I also wonder how sincere their words are. Do they really want to serve me in any way that they can? Do they really wish for me to rule long?

The ceremony is about wrapped up. Nash comes up to the dais again, his gaze intent on mine. When he's beside me, in front of the table holding the chalice, he stops and faces the crowd. He holds out his fist, arm in a straight line, angled toward the crowd. "To Queen Ryn."

The crowd mimics his gesture, raising their fists in the air. They cry out in massive roar, "To Queen Ryn."

I am officially over my people.

I only hope I don't bungle it up.

CHAPTER 14

"YOU ARE OFFICIALLY THE QUEEN," *the First Queen says.* "What plans do you have now?"

"I don't know. I should look into the laws more. Help my people. I like the idea of meeting with them. Having them come to me. I want to make certain that happens."

"It's a good goal to have."

But is it enough?

"It will be, as long as you are trying your best."

"I don't know. I have a hard time making decisions that affect my people so much. I want to do right by them, but I'm also afraid of messing up."

"Remember what I told you before. It's all right for the queen to make mistakes."

We discuss more than what feels like fluff, but that's what my world keeps coming back to—it's all right for me to make mistakes. It doesn't feel that way.

The colors of the sunset fade as we say goodbye. They stay with me though, in my heart.

I wake to find Inkga entering the room.

"You're sleeping late this morning," she says.

I stretch and hop out of bed. "It won't happen again."

She shakes her head with a smile. "There's no reason for you to explain yourself. You can sleep in as much as you'd like. You've earned it."

"I'm not accustomed to it." Strange to think one day I might be.

I hurry to throw on a pair of black pants and a deep-blue blouse, stash my weapons, check to make certain I have my poison pouch around my neck, and let Inkga do my hair before she excuses herself with a smile.

I'm eager to see Nash.

A servant brings me breakfast, and I eat, barely tasting my food. The whole time I expect Nash to interrupt me, but he never does. He must be busy this morning. There is a lot for him to do, though usually he includes me in his duties.

He'll be by soon.

I pace the room. At some point a servant comes to take my tray away, but Nash still doesn't appear. Time to go find him. Maybe I'll finally get that stroll through the gardens.

I step out to find Wilric, Afet, Stird, and a female guard I don't recognize. They follow me as I go through the palace. He's not in the council room nor the room I sometimes meet in with my ladies-in-waiting, and I don't find him in the throne room or the Mortum Tura room with its many mirrors reflecting nothing back to me but myself.

He's probably waiting for me back in my room. It was silly to leave. I was so anxious to see him, though.

Lengthening my stride, I hurry toward my rooms. My escorts keep pace, staying silent. I'm almost getting used to having someone with me wherever I go. *Almost.* I open my door with a grin on my face.

No one's here.

I suppress a frown as I turn to the servant always waiting by my room. "Please go fetch my Head Advisor for me."

"Yes, Your Majesty." He gives a bow and hurries off to go do my bidding.

What could be keeping Nash? He's usually here before I even think of him. It's likely that he's got things on his schedule this morning, but usually I come first.

I go in my sitting room and pace.

I tap my fingers against my legs.

I want to see his face.

Brush my fingertips against his.

I huff, impatient for things to be moving along. I can't wait for him all day; I have duties I need to attend to now that I'm officially the queen. I want to meet with my people and fix laws. Standing here all day isn't allowed.

What feels like a good hour later, there's a knock. I grin, open the door, and my face falls. It's the servant I sent to find him, and he's alone except for the guards.

"Forgive me, Your Majesty," he says with a bow. "I can't find your Head Advisor anywhere."

My gut burns. "What do you mean, you can't find him?"

He shirks back, voice meek. "I mean, he's nowhere to be found. No one has seen him since he went to bed last night."

"That can't be. He was supposed to meet me here this morning. Look again."

"Yes, Your Highness." He bows once more and rushes away while I remain with the doorway with my escorts.

I drum my fingers on my thigh. "Wilric, do you know where Nash's mother lives?"

"I do, Your Majesty."

"Please go to his home and see if he needed to visit his family." Perhaps an emergency turned up. I'll have to tell him to send a note to me next time this happens. I hope everything is all right with them.

"Yes, my lady." Wilric sets off.

I go back to pacing, this time keeping my door open. I'm

anxious to find out what Nash has to say for himself. What excuse he has for not checking in with me. I cluck my tongue. His disappearance is inexcusable. There's no reason for him not to let me know what's going on, even with a quick note.

My pacing becomes frenzied as time passes. It's hard not to watch the clock on my wall tick by slowly, edging forward like it hasn't a care in the world. It doesn't understand my need for it to move more quickly. To get answers about Nash.

Half an hour later, the servant returns, huffing for air.

"Well?" I demand.

"I'm sorry, Your Majesty. There's no sign of him. I have half the servants and some guards as well out, looking for him."

How can this possibly be? He must have gone home early in the morning. "Send me one of the guards who was on duty at the portcullis this morning."

"Yes, my lady."

After he leaves, I pull out a non-poisoned dagger and clean my fingernails with it. By the time I'm done, not only does the guard show up, but he also has Jaku at his side.

"Did you see Nash leave the palace grounds this morning?" I spit out.

"No, my lady. There's been very little activity at the gate this morning," the guard says.

"Where is he?" My voice is a roar.

"Forgive me, Your Majesty," Jaku says with a head bow. "I understand your need for your Head Advisor. This isn't like him at all, but I'm sure it's nothing. We'll find him."

"You understand nothing." My heart squeezes, a painful, choking feeling.

"I will personally go search for him and have my men on the lookout." Jaku doesn't wait for an answer, but bows and turns to leave with the guard.

I growl. My stomach is churning—an awful, gut wrenching

feeling. Where could he be? It's been hours since I should have seen him. This is ridiculous. I need him.

My eyes threaten to water. I blink. Now is not the time to give in to weakness.

I have to find him.

A thought hits me with such force, I gasp. What if he left me? What if he realized how awful I truly am? How stained my soul is? How much blood is on my hands?

He couldn't take being around me any longer.

I tighten my grip around my dagger.

It can't be, but why else would he have disappeared?

He wouldn't leave his family, though. He'll be there, and then I can demand answers. Demand that he at least turn in a resignation before running away.

Unless something has happened to his family.

My jaw aches from my clenching it so tight.

There's a commotion out in the hall. I race to my doorway, where my guards are blocking three women with Wilric from entering. As soon as Wilric spots me, he says, "Nash's family."

I recognize the two younger women as his sisters. "Bring them in."

"But we need to check them for weapons," Afet says.

"Bring them in now." My voice silences everyone.

I take to the corner, from where I can watch both the door and the window. Nash's sisters and the woman I assume is his mother hurry in the room. They begin talking over one another, with Wilric silent next to them. The muscle in his jaw is tense.

I raise a hand to quiet them.

They do so and curtsy.

"Forgive us, Your Majesty," Nash's mother says. She has graying hair and Nash's blue-specked hazel eyes. "We're worried about Nash. Have you heard?"

That makes me worry all the more. My heart pounds harder with each word Wilric says.

"Nash was not at home. His mother and sisters are certain he would have stayed true to his duty to you or sent you advance notice if he was called away."

A flash of heat zips through me. "Where could he be?" My voice is faint. Weak.

"We were hoping you could help us find the answer to that question," his mother says.

How can I? I have nothing for her.

"Is there any place you know of he might visit? Any haunt he enjoys?" I ask.

"Only here and home," she says. "He's committed to work and doesn't do much else."

I'm working him too hard. "When was the last time you saw him?"

"Four days ago, Your Majesty."

I open my mouth to speak, when Jaku enters the room. "He's nowhere to be seen. What's more, I found evidence of a struggle in his room."

My heart drops to the center of the world. "What type of evidence?"

His gaze skirts to the women in the room before returning to me. "There were drops of blood on the floor."

I want to collapse.

Nash has been taken.

CHAPTER 15

"How can that be?" Nash's mother asks, voice shaking.

"I've got to search his room," I say.

"My lady, forgive me, but I'm not certain it's safe," Jaku says. "I need to secure the room and the perimeter around it better first, to make certain it's safe."

"I can protect myself." I flash my dagger.

"I know you can, but I would be remiss if I didn't check anyway."

"Fine. But do it now. I want to see the scene before much time passes."

He bows and is gone.

Guilt hits me. He went missing under my watch. And it has to be Daros. Who else would it be, unless I have an enemy I'm unaware of?

That's entirely likely too. I don't know what to do. I need to see his room, to get answers.

I did this to his family.

"Your Majesty," a servant says, entering the room, "the council wishes to see you."

"Now?" There couldn't be a worse time for it.

"They requested now, Your Majesty. They say it has to do with your missing Head Advisor."

Maybe they somehow got the answers I was unable to find. "Have someone take care of Nash's family for me." I turn to them. "I will be back as soon as I can. We will figure this out."

The mother nods. The girls just look frightened.

I hurry out of the room, unwilling to waste another minute.

It takes longer than I'd like to get through the hallways to the council room, though I'm going at top speed. My escorts follow, armor clanking.

When I get to the council room, all council members and their aides are here.

"What news do you have of Nash?" The words are out of me as soon as everyone bows.

I don't bother sitting; I stand behind my usual seat.

"It's not that we have news of him," Timit says. "With blood in his room and him missing, we need things fixed. We need you to choose a new Head Advisor."

This has to be a joke. There's no way I can pick one under these circumstances. "I will not."

"You have to," Yuka says, but her words are soft. "The law states that you must have one present at all times, in case something happens to you. We can't let our country fall into disarray."

"I don't want to."

"What if someone was to kill you?" Timit asks.

"No one will." Though my voice is low, it fills the room.

"I understand this is hard," Yuka says, "but you have to choose someone. We can't leave it up to chance."

I say the first name that comes to mind. "My lady-in-waiting, Jem Surha." Where did that come from? It doesn't matter. She won't be in the position long. "Now, if you'll excuse me, I need to go find my real Head Advisor."

"You can't pick a lady-in-waiting," Kada says.

"Why not?"

"Because she's a lady-in-waiting, not an advisor," Timit says.

"And she advises me in that form. Might as well do it as my Head Advisor until Nash gets back." I still don't know why I said her name. Ranen, Borkus, and Freya were going to control her—she admitted herself that they might have had power over her. So why do I trust her all of the sudden?

Jem acted differently around the people. She's been more thoughtful and less snide lately. She might make an all right regent until a new queen was chosen, if she didn't let others control her. Not that I have any intention of dying and making her so.

It doesn't matter. There are more important things to do.

"If Her Majesty wishes to name Jem her Head Advisor, she can do so," Mina says.

The others scoff, and I have to wonder if it's because she's one of those farthest from my seat. Her advice isn't supposed to mean as much as that of people closer to me, but I appreciate it. "Thank you."

They continue to argue, but I leave the room.

Jaku is waiting when I get back to my room. "The room is ready for your inspection."

"Thank you for being so swift."

I follow him, not knowing where I'm going. I should know where Nash sleeps, but all I know is that it's in the bunkhouse with the other guards. I need to see his family after this. I can't leave them hanging; they have more of a right to information than I do.

We wind through hallways and out of the building and come to a complex that looks small next to the palace, but is fairly big in reality.

"This is where all the guards sleep," Jaku says.

"Where are Nash's quarters?" The words bite out of me.

"This way." He doesn't hesitate.

We pass by one brick building and enter a second.

"This is where I moved him shortly after he became Head Advisor. He said he needed to stay with the men, but I insisted that he needed a space at least somewhat more befitting his station, since he refused to move into the palace."

There are guards around, some stationed and others looking at the ground as if searching for something. The floor is a rough wood, smoothed by what must have been years of use. The walls are wood too, with no decorations on them.

"What is this place?" I ask.

"It's where the leaders of the guard sleep. My personal quarters are through here. I saw and heard nothing out of the usual last night or this morning."

We pass several rooms, people all over the place. How could anyone have snuck out of here with Nash, without someone seeing them? I ask Jaku just that.

"There weren't as many guards around this morning. They are here now both to look for more clues and for your safety. It must have been in the middle of the night when he was taken, for nobody to have noticed. Though even then, shifts are always changing."

That's not a good sign. Nash wouldn't have left without a fight if he could help it.

What did they do to him?

My stomach rolls as I follow Jaku. He stops next to a room and motions me inside.

"Take all the time you need." He stands inside the door frame. There's another guard outside the window, his back to us.

I'm overly aware of being in Nash's room—of how this is his space—but I can't dwell on it when his life may hang in the balance.

"Where's the blood?" I ask.

"It's over there, by the bed, on the floor. There are a few drops."

Thank goodness there isn't more, but that doesn't mean it wasn't spilled.

There's a bed, a dresser, and a washbasin with a clouded mirror over it. Simple furnishings. It doesn't surprise me. The walls are bare, but there are plenty of blankets on the bed. The bed that's unmade doesn't seem right.

"Does he usually leave his bed unmade?"

"I wouldn't know. I make it a point to give the officers, including him, as much privacy as possible, though our guards are taught to keep things clean."

Not helpful, but understandable. Nash was most likely taken during the night.

I inch closer to the bed, studying the floor. Then I see it—a drop of red. And another.

It's not much, but it's enough.

My heart gives a painful squeeze.

I get on my hands and knees to look underneath the bed.

"What are you doing, Your Majesty? One of us can do that for you."

I ignore him. It's dark, but there's nothing here. Nash keeps this place immaculate.

Just thinking of him hurts.

I swipe my hand all the way under the bed to make sure I'm not missing anything. When nothing comes up, I get up and scour the room, looking over every nook and cranny, opening his drawers and riffling through his things.

I don't even feel bad about it.

But it does no good.

There's nothing out of the ordinary.

I look in the wash basin. Nothing. I fling the blankets off the bed and go through them one at a time. I search under the pillow. Still nothing.

I have no clue as to where he's gone, but there has to be something. I go over the floor again and again. Finally, I shut the door and search behind it. There's a glint in one of the cracks. I did out my dagger and chip away at the wood around it until it's loose. A gem.

My throat closes up as I reach for it.

It's cold in my hand.

It looks exactly like one of the gems on the hilt of Daros's knife.

I was right, and it's never felt so horrid. Not only is Nash gone, but Daros came for him personally.

Nash doesn't have a chance.

CHAPTER 16

I HESITATE outside the room my guards have placed Nash's family in. I sent word to the council, but this is going to be much harder. What does one say to a family when their son has been taken by the cruelest man alive?

I don't know.

I steady myself and go inside, my escorts staying outside.

"He's gone, isn't he?" Nash's mother says before I can form any words.

"He's been taken. I'm sorry." Though that doesn't say nearly enough. Doesn't do nearly enough. I've brought this pain on them.

I should have killed Daros when I had the chance.

"It's not your fault," she says with a sob. She grabs onto her closest daughter and heaves out wretched cries of anguish.

His sisters are oddly quiet, though tears stream down their faces. I wish there was something I could do to comfort all three of them.

But there's not.

It's much too late for that.

What happened in the past doesn't matter. Only how we handle the future does. If he's taken, he may not be dead yet. "I will find him and bring him back, whatever it takes." Even if he's dead by that point. I gulp past the tightness of my throat.

His mother calms, though she doesn't stop crying.

"We've got our best men out looking for him," I say. "I've ordered the military and off-duty guards to go look for him. I even ordered some guards on duty to stop and look for him." They won't find him, though.

Daros will never be found unless he wants to.

The same now holds true for Nash, unless Daros wants me to find them both. The thought sends a wave of chills down my back.

"How will you find him?" Her shoulders are hunched in on themselves.

That's a good question. "I'll tear apart all of Valcora if I have to." And I mean it.

"I'm sure you'll find him, then." Though tempered by the waver in her voice, her words hold confidence.

How can I break that?

How can I tell her the truth? "You must know we believe him to have been taken by an escaped convict, intent on hurting me. Hopefully, that means nothing will happen to Nash while the criminal tries to do what he wants with me."

She breaks into a new round of tears, her daughters oscillating between comforting her and being upset themselves. When she gets a hold of herself, she says, "Forgive me for not introducing myself, Your Majesty. I am Slipa."

"Nash has talked about you before. Said good things." It's all I can come up with to say to this woman. I have no words of comfort, to ease the pain.

"Good. I'd have words with him if he didn't, when he got back."

I open my mouth, unsure what to say.

Before I can speak, she says through her tears, "Don't tell me any different. He's talked a lot about your abilities. His faith in you. I have to believe that, if anyone can find him, you can."

I choke.

"Are you all right?" She moves to pat me on the back before pulling her hand back like it was bitten.

She must have remembered the law.

No one can comfort me.

I choke back my feelings. "Please let my servants know if you need anything. I've arranged for you to have guards on your family at all times."

Just in case.

"Oh, we don't need that. We'll be safe at home."

"You will accept them and keep them with you." My voice is firmer than I meant, but I'm not backing down.

Daros could take one of them as a way to torture Nash.

Nash. What must he be going through?

I turn my head so they don't see the tears pooling in my eyes. Once I get a hold of myself, I say, "I will keep you updated as things progress."

"That would be appreciated. Please let us know if there's anything we can do," Slipa says.

I nod, wishing there was something they could do.

They curtsy, Slipa and the girls' cheeks still wet with tears.

I leave the room, unable to bear any more. I have to find some way to accomplish the impossible—and get Nash back.

CHAPTER 17

I RUB my temple with my thumb. Now would be the time to talk to Nash, instead of stewing by myself in my sitting room. To see his take on the subject. That's impossible when he's the missing subject.

I have everyone out looking for him. I gave them a list of places Daros is known to frequent. People he knows. But I know they won't find anything, unless Daros wants them to.

How did Daros know to take Nash? How did he know Nash meant more to me than anyone else? It's a mystery. Daros did everything he could to train the humanity out of me. What could have possibly clued him in to the fact my heart has softened toward Nash? Still, I should have known better than to let my feelings out. I would rather Daros took me instead.

But maybe that's the point.

I can handle these things. Did my whole life. Knowing someone I care about is going through them instead is tearing my guts apart. Makes me want to scream.

I bite my lip until I taste blood.

There's a knock, and I rush to it, hoping for news about Nash. All I need is him, safe and sound by my side.

But when I answer, it's Jem.

I leave the door open without a greeting and go sit in my chair in the corner.

She enters, taking her time. I expect her to pick the seat as far from me as possible, but she surprises me by sitting right next to me.

"I'm sorry they took him." Her voice is soft.

I grunt. What else am I supposed to do? Being sorry won't fix anything. I need him found. Need him back here. Safe.

When I don't respond, she says, "I heard you made me your new Head Advisor."

Mention of that makes my head spin. I put my head in my hands, willing the world to stop tilting.

"I don't know how hard this must be for you, but we have to keep the government running. We can't let it fall apart because one person was taken."

"One person? It wasn't just *one person*. It was Nash." I raise my voice before I can stop myself. I continue anyway. "You have no idea what Daros will do to him. What pain and torture will be inflicted upon him."

She shrinks back in her chair. I bite my lip again, once again tasting blood. As much as I'm right, she has a point.

I can't let myself fall apart.

My people are counting on me.

Even if I can't count on myself.

"It's been a rough day." It's the best I can do, to apologize.

"I can't imagine."

I look at her. Really look. She has a contrite expression—soft eyes and down-turned lips. I believe her.

"What now?" she asks.

What would Nash want me to do? "We still need to arrange for me to meet with the people. Having them come to the throne room is a good idea. Make sure the ladies-in-waiting are organizing it." It's a wise move. Whoever took him is going to be watching for my reaction. Carrying on is the best thing I can do.

"Consider it done. Do you want to meet with the council like normal?" she asks. "Or should I cancel that?"

"I should go." It's strange to be speaking with her like this. To hear her words so similar to Nash's. No sneer in her voice. No snide remarks. "Why are you being so kind and helpful?" I ask.

She drops her gaze to her hands, a faint stain of pink on her cheeks. "I should have been so, from the beginning. But I'm determined not to let you down, now that I'm your Head Advisor."

Hmm. "Why were you rude at first?"

She curls her hands together to form one tense ball. "I'm sorry, Your Majesty."

"I don't want apologies. I want a reason."

She takes a deep breath. "Because you were a nobody, who cut your way through us to drink the Mortum Tura. Because I was jealous of your bravery. Because I didn't want to become queen but knew it was my duty to try."

The First Queen told me not wanting the power of becoming queen would become so. Jem would have become queen then, had I not drank first. "Would you have let Ranen and Faya control you?"

"Probably." She presses her lips together tightly. "I didn't realize how bad they were. How self-serving they were. How much they wanted control of the kingdom. To me they were always nice and helped me learn the ways of court. Ranen didn't treat me like he treated you."

I can't believe she trusted them. I saved the country from being ruled by power-hungry people. But does it matter? I may not be power hungry, but now I'm obsessed with finding Nash. I can't imagine that's much better. In both cases, the good of the country comes second. "I'll forgive you for acting that way if you forgive me for being so rude."

Her eyebrows shoot upward as she widens her eyes. "A queen doesn't have to apologize for anything."

"If you haven't noticed, I'm not one to stand on conventions."

A smile works its way across her mouth. "I've noticed. Very well. I forgive you and will strive harder in the future to be kinder to you."

I think we understand each other better than we did before. My heart still hurts for Nash, though.

There's a knock, and without being prompted, Jem answers it. This meeting shows she does know her place, while I'm floundering to find mine.

Jem says, "It's a note, Your Majesty."

The servant walks in, bows, and hands me a note that's bulky before leaving. Something's in the envelope that's sealed with wax decorated with nothing but a circle.

I open it with trembling fingers, wondering if it's news or something mundane. Inside, there are not only words from his captors, but also Nash's ring, the silver dotted with blood.

I clasp it in my fist, wishing more than anything that I could take his place.

If you ever want to see your Head Advisor alive again, do as you're told. You will lower taxes for the Kurah to almost nothing and raise them for everyone else back to how they were. Fail to do this within the hour, and he will be the one to pay.

I hurry to the door and throw it open with a crash. "Who sent this?"

A servant cowers in the middle of all my guards. He's vaguely familiar from a few moments ago. He looks at his feet. "I brought it, Your Majesty."

"Where did you get it from?"

"It was given to the guards at the portcullis by a little boy, Your Highness." His voice quivers.

I slam my door shut. They're not going to find who it came from. "I have to meet with the council. Now." My voice fills the room as I clutch the note and ring to me. I have to prevent Nash from coming to any more harm, even if it means raising taxes on those I most want to help. Can I pretend to raise taxes and then change them? Probably not, since taxes are paid weekly, something I should have changed. Now it's too late.

Why would Daros want this? What is his plan? How will he know I'll stick to it after Nash is free? It makes my stomach curdle.

CHAPTER 18

I HURRY along to the council room while Jem and my escorts walk around me. Jem's reading the note while I slip Nash's ring on my thumb. I will keep it safe. I'll keep him safe. And then, when he returns, I'll give it back to him.

I just don't know how much else it'll take to heal him.

I haven't healed yet myself from my years with Daros.

"You can't follow through with this," Jem says as we rush through the hallways.

I glare at her. "What do you mean, I can't?"

"If you give into their demands, everyone will know you can be persuaded by outside influences and how to manipulate you."

"But if I don't do this, Nash will die."

She hesitates. "They could be bluffing."

"Daros isn't the type to bluff."

"I don't mean to be insensitive, and I know it's hard, but a queen cannot give in to blackmail."

She's right; I can't allow this to affect me. I'm not sure how to do that, though. "Will you have a servant fetch Nash's family?"

"Right away."

It takes some time for them to come, and I think of what to tell them. Of what I should do. When they come in, they have red-rimmed, puffy eyes. I avert my gaze. "Please, be seated."

They pick seats nearby. His mother, Slipa, is the first to speak. "Is there news of him? Is he coming back?"

I have to shatter the hope in her eyes. I wish I didn't. "If I don't lower taxes for the Kurah and up them for the Poruah and Medi in the next half hour or so, the person that holds Nash is going to hurt him."

Lanay's mouth forms an O. She says, "You're going to do what they say, yes?"

"Lanay, the queen will do what's best. We aren't to question her."

Slipa looks at me unwaveringly.

I can't hold her gaze. "I can't give into them." But oh, how I want to.

Belta surprises me by getting down on her knees. "Please, Your Majesty. *Please.* I'll do anything if you give in to their demands. We can't go on without my brother. We can't lose him like we lost our father." She clasps her hands together, eyes filled to the brim with tears.

How can I deny her what my heart wants? At the same time, how can I say *yes*? I can fix the taxes back after Nash returns, right? So what's stopping me from doing everything I can to get him back and maybe find Daros in the process? He'll let his guard down if he thinks I'm complying, and I'll get both him and Nash—Daros to go to the chopping block and Nash back on my side.

Daros has to know I'll consider this, though. Why would he ask me to change something I can just change back later? I don't have an answer to that, but I know what I'm going to do. "I'll take care of your brother."

Belta collapses backward, only to be picked up by Lanay, who says, "Thank you, Your Majesty. Thank you. Thank you. You don't know how much this means to us."

Because of my feelings for Nash, I may have an inkling.

"You will get him back, won't you?" Slipa looks so weak, like she's lost ten pounds since I last saw her. Like she's losing her strength to fight with her son in an evil man's hands.

"I will." I put all the conviction I can in those words, even if I don't entirely believe them.

I stand, and they jump to their feet. I see them out and head to the council room to make the change before I decide this isn't a good idea.

"See that Nash's family gets home safely," I say to the closest guard.

"Yes, Your Highness."

"Your Majesty." Jem appears from behind one of the guards waiting outside my rooms. "Where are you going?"

"To change the taxes."

"You can't do that."

I stop and turn toward her so fast one of my guards almost runs into me. "I will do this. Nothing you say will stop me."

I stride on. She doesn't follow for a moment but eventually catches up to me. Only this time, she stays silent.

The council room is only half-full of people left from the last meeting. Those here bow or curtsy. I tell them to rise as I take a seat. I don't care for social norms usually—less so today. "I want the rest of the council here in five minutes, or we're starting without them."

Servants at the edges of the room scramble out, no doubt to tell those not here what kind of mood I'm in. Fine by me. The sooner we get this taken care of, the sooner Nash will be safe.

If I'm going to do this, I want to make certain it works.

Time ticks by, like a dagger repeatedly thrown in the wrong spot. It does no good to watch the clock or listen to those murmuring around me. I want this done and over with. People are trickling in, but not fast enough.

As I wait, I survey each person in the room. Who here is a traitor? Which of them are going to report to Daros what I say here today? It could be any of them. *All* of them.

No. I'm getting carried away. If it was all of them, Daros would have an easy enough time killing me and putting someone pliable on the throne. I glace at Jem out of the corner of my eye. Is she still pliable, or would she stick up for herself now? She certainly isn't afraid to tell me what she thinks.

Four minutes. Close enough to five, though we're still missing a few people.

Without preamble, I say, "I am reverting the taxes. Not just that, but I'm lowering them further for the Kurah."

Timit gives a smug smile. "This will make our economy grow. You are wiser than your years, my lady."

I ignore his flattery. He might as well be the one working with Daros, as far as I'm concerned. And he never reported back to me on the finances and whether my plan would sustain the country. Do leaders of other countries have this many problems?

"But, Your Highness," Yuka says, "the people are so excited about the changes you made. I ask that you please reconsider."

"Not everyone is excited," Kada says.

"It's true. I think many will be much happier after this change." Timit's sausage lips turn upward.

"It doesn't matter what the people think," I say, wishing it were true. "This law is changing."

Several council members talk over one another. I silence them all. "We're done arguing about this. It's happening. Timit, I want the word spread within half an hour in Indell and as soon as horses can be sent to the rest of the country."

"But, Your Majesty, these things take time."

I bang my fist on the table. "Get it done."

"Yes, Your Highness. If you will excuse me, I have people I need to speak with."

I never thought I'd see him run, but after a quick bow, that's exactly what he does.

"Any questions?" My voice is rough. Jaded. "Good," I say when nobody speaks.

"My lady," Mina's voice is fain.

"What is it?"

"I'm afraid we can't continue to have the army and guards out looking for Nash Zorris. I know he was your Head Advisor, and we all respect that, but it's putting too great of a strain on the country to have so many of our people out looking for him."

There are murmurs of agreement.

We need to save him, but how do I make them to understand it? "I get that it's a strain, but what would you want me to do if you were the one kidnapped?" I look each of them in the eyes, ignoring the guilt that has me wondering if I would do the same for them. "Would you want me to leave you there, because it's inconvenient?"

They look away but don't say anything.

"That settles it. I'm not going to let the kidnappers get away with this. We will find Nash, and we will bring those who took him to justice." If only my words were true. It's hard to believe them.

As I head back toward my rooms, I can't help but think maybe they're right. I am putting Nash before my country. Before everything.

But I don't know what else to do.

CHAPTER 19

As I walk through the halls, I can't help wondering if that was enough to save Nash's life. It might not be the right thing to do, but I'm going to stick to it.

There's no guarantee Daros will hold up to his end of the bargain. There's no telling he's not doing things to harm Nash. I'd stake my life on the fact that Daros is torturing him. Even without the blood on his ring, I'd know that.

Daros won't be doing the deed himself. He has others for that. Though that does beg the question—why was his jewel in Nash's room to begin with? Why would Daros stoop to kidnapping Nash himself? Because I know he didn't give that knife to anyone; it wouldn't leave his hands.

What's done is done. I hope they aren't pushing him past his breaking point.

Jem enters my sitting room after me. I should have known she wouldn't let things go.

"What do you need?" I ask.

She gives a curtsy. She does that much too frequently. "I want to help, Your Majesty. What can I do?"

I lift an eyebrow, not certain if there's more to it. I'm going to utilize her anyway, because she's offering and because I need extra hands. "I would like to send a note to Nash's family. Would you please write what I dictate?" I could write it myself, but it'd take a lot longer and be harder to read.

"Let me get some paper and ink, and I will do as you ask."

As she goes out, I say to the nearest servant in the hall, "Send for Jaku. I want to speak with him as soon as I'm done with Jem. Also, I will need one of my ladies-in-waiting, along with a couple of guards."

"Yes, Your Majesty." The servant hurries off, hopefully to carry out my will.

I return to my room. There are so many memories here. So much life. Nash and I almost always talked in here. He taught me. Was patient with me. Helped me.

We fought in here, both verbally and physically. I wish I'd never argued with him, but I miss the sparring. I didn't do a good enough job teaching him if they were able to get to him and drag him off.

The thought of him suffering brings me to my knees. I pull on my hair with a growl. They can't do this. I'll never forgive myself for not killing Daros when I had the chance. So what if I made a promise to myself never to kill again?

It was a stupid promise.

The door opens. I don't move from my spot.

"Your Majesty, what are you doing on the floor?" Jem rushes to my side.

I point at the low table, pretending it's normal to be caught down here. "You can write there."

She draws her eyebrows together and opens her mouth to say something, but stops herself. She scoots over to the low table, opting to sit on the floor as well. No doubt she finds it offensive that I would make her do this, but I don't have enough energy to budge.

"What would you like me to write?" she asks, quill ready.

I dictate slowly, thinking about what to say and giving her time to write.

Dear Slipa,

In regards to your son, I am extending every effort to bring him back to us.

I want to say *in one piece*, but that's not a promise I can make. I'm not sure I should be offering either of us any hope, but I have to do what I can.

I went ahead and changed the taxes as requested. I am doing so in the hopes they will return him to us soon, though I have no guarantee. Please rest assured that I am doing everything in my power. Nash will come back to us. I will make certain of it."

I stop before I make more promises I can't keep and sign my name. A name I have because Nash encouraged me to pick one out.

I choke back a sob.

Jem doesn't seem to notice. She folds up the note and seals it. "I will get this sent immediately."

When I've gotten control of myself, I say, "No. I requested a lady-in-waiting and some guards to deliver it. I want to make certain Nash's mother gets it and that she knows how personally invested I am in finding her son."

Jem taps the letter on her hand. "I understand you care for him, but you can't devote everything we have into finding him."

I turn toward the window, squeezing my eyes shut against the pain. "You've made yourself clear."

The tapping sounds a few more times, followed by her faint footsteps. The door opens. I blink a few times before facing her and those who entered. Pina, my youngest lady in waiting, is in the hall with several more guards than usual and Jaku.

"Jem has a letter that needs to be delivered to Nash's mother," I tell Pina. "Wilric will give your guards directions to find her home. Please deliver it and offer her my personal apologizes for being unable to bring it myself."

"Yes, Your Majesty." Pina curtseys and takes the note from Jem before hurrying away.

"Jaku, enter. Jem, it's up to you whether you stay or not."

She skirts back into the room, following Jaku.

"Give me an update," I tell Jaku.

His mouth is a grim line, his eyes sad. "I'm sorry, Your Majesty. I have no news to report as of yet."

I want to punch something.

Jem speaks up. "What are you doing to search for him?"

Jaku slides his gaze to me before returning it to Jem. "We have men out in the entire city, looking."

"That's it?" Jem asks when he doesn't say more. "What about the countryside? What about other cities? Indell is not the only place they could be keeping him."

Why haven't we been looking for him farther out? I'm so used to Daros working in the city, I hadn't thought outside of that.

"Forgive me, but we don't have enough men for that. Even now, my guards are stretched thin."

I clear my throat. It's raw and I don't want to talk, but I force myself. "Don't stretch yourselves any thinner. I don't want anyone else hurt or taken while we're looking for him. Send word to the guards in other cities and alert them to the possibility Nash could be with them. They should keep an eye out for him."

"Yes, Your Majesty," he says. "Is there anything else you recommend we do?"

I glance out the window. I wish I knew a way to bring him back to me. "No."

"If that's all, then I will get back to work. I'll let you know if I have anything to report."

I dismiss him, and with a bow, he leaves the room.

It's silent after he leaves.

What do you say when someone you care about deeply has been taken?

Jem's words are faint. "Maybe it's for the best."

"What is?" My voice is dead.

"That he's gone."

"For the best?" That makes me roar to life. *"For the best?* Get out of my sight. Get out, right now."

"I'm sorry, Your Majesty," she says as she backs up. "You just seem very attached to him, and you know the queen can't afford to be."

"You have no idea what they're doing to him. What kind of pain he has to be in."

Her eyes widen. "Forgive me. I misspoke."

"I said *get out.*"

She scurries for the door and slams it behind her.

I can't believe she said that.

Can't believe Nash is gone.

I bury my face in my hands and cry.

CHAPTER 20

SOMETIME AFTER MY eyes have dried, there's a knock.

"Enter," I say.

The door squeaks open. There's a hesitation, and then Pina says, "Your Majesty, I have a note back from Nash's mother."

I pull myself to my feet, and Pina hands me the note. It's not bulky like the last one. No hidden ring with blood on it.

I want to gag. Instead, I take deep breaths as I open the letter.

QUEEN RYN,

Thank you for your kind words about my son. I know you will do what you can to find him. I love him dearly and want nothing more than his return. Thank you for doing everything you can to bring him back to me.

Your faithful servant,
Slipa

HER WORDS HURT. Am I really doing what's best for him? What's best for my people? What would he want? Would he want me to let him... die?

I swallow against the pain and the memories.

Should I change the taxes back again? There's still time. There's always time. Timit won't be happy—many of the council won't—but then, they'll be glad I'm not using more of our resources for Nash.

But I can't do it.

Slipa and his sisters are in such pain. They care for him so much—more than anyone ever cared for me.

It might be a mercy to let him die and not have to put up with the torture. Then again, do I really know what they're doing to him? Maybe the blood was just to scare me. Maybe there's more going on than meets the eyes.

I don't know what to do.

I wish Nash was here to advise me. The next best thing is the First Queen. I need only go to sleep, and she'll be there waiting for me. She'll help. I know she will. There has to be some sort of magic that can be used to locate a person. It's time we stopped being so afraid of using magic.

Pina is still here.

"Thank you for doing your duty. Go get some dinner, and I'll see you tomorrow," I say.

"Aren't you going to eat?" she asks.

"I'm not hungry."

She looks like she wants to protest but doesn't dare. Good. I'm not up for another argument.

"If you're sure... I'll see you in the morning, Your Highness." She curtseys, and I nod for her to leave.

Once I'm alone, I deflate. I can barely pretend to be strong when people are around. When they're gone, I'm a mess.

How did I let this happen?

I force myself through exercises I can do in my room before I hurry to change into a night gown and huddle up on the bed to force sleep to come. Too much time passes with me still awake. How will I get aid from the First Queen if I can't rest?

A knock sounds. I yell, "Come in."

Inkga enters. "I didn't realize you wished to go to bed. You should have rang for me, and I would have come helped."

"I didn't feel like bothering you."

"I know you didn't eat anything off of your tray earlier. Would you like me to order you dinner?" Though her voice is soft, it grates on me.

I shake my head.

"Do you want me to sit with you for a while?"

I want to tell her *no*, but what comes out is, "I'd like that."

When did I get so weak as to want people around? I don't know, but I can't say I entirely regret it. I don't want to be alone at a moment like this, when all of me feels as if I will come crashing down on myself, and I can't seem to sleep and get the advice I so desperately need.

She pulls the chair from my vanity over to the bedside while I sit up, resting my back against the headboard. It's awkward. I've not had a person around to comfort me like this before. I don't know what to say or do. Whatever it is, I need something to distract me.

"Tell me about your family." The words come out before I've thought of them.

She takes it in stride. "What do you want to know?"

"Anything. Everything."

She nods like she understands, but I'm not sure anyone can.

"I believe you know my mother," she says.

"I do?" This surprises me. I know so few people.

"Monkia."

"The Head of Staff is your mother?"

"She is. That's how I got a job in the palace to begin with. They are very sought-after positions, and I wouldn't have been able to acquire the job were it not for her."

A smile tugs at my lips. "Funny. I'm not sure if she really likes me or not."

"There's no question that she does. Whether or not she goes with you on the council, though, is a different matter."

"How do you know she likes me?"

"I don't know if she did at first, but now there's a note of respect in her voice when she talks about you."

"Weird."

She laughs. "Extra weird for me. Who do I listen to when you two have differing opinions? The queen or my mother?"

That almost makes me laugh along with her. "I won't fault you for agreeing with your mother. Did you help her with the ball?"

"Not much. Mostly, I listened to her talk about it when she came home at night."

"You two share a room, then?" I ask.

"We share living quarters in the servants' area. She could have had a place in the palace, but we both like it better away from the hubbub of the palace."

I wonder what that means. "What about the rest of your family? Or is it you and your mom?"

"Nope. My dad works at the palace too. He's head of the horses in the stables."

"Do you have any brothers or sisters?"

"I don't."

"So working at the palace is a family affair. Does your father get to stay in the same quarters as you and your mother?"

"No. He stays with the men."

This I don't understand. "Do we not have living quarters for families?"

"You don't."

"Maybe I should remedy this."

"Trust me, if there's anything the queen shouldn't worry about, it's this. My parents get along much better when they're not together."

That's a sad thought, but at least she has her parents. I never had any—unless you count Daros as an adoptive parent, which I don't.

"It's a good thing, really. I can visit my father in the stables whenever I'm not busy, and I get to see my mom at night. I have both my parents near me, which is more than a lot of servants can say."

It sounds almost like a dream. I can't imagine anything like that. "What's it like, having your parents around?"

"It's…" She shrugs. "Just what it is. I like having them close, though I'm old enough I should be making my way in the world. I don't know what it is about family, but it makes me feel safe. Like I belong. Happy. I wish I could share that with you."

"I wish you could too." My voice is so faint that I'm not sure she hears me.

"Don't you know anything about your family? Is that why you told the ladies-in-waiting not to bring them to the palace?"

She's rather forward for a servant, but I'm not about to argue with her when I'm so exhausted. "I don't know anything about my family. I was left as a baby to Daros. And now he has Nash."

The room goes silent.

I'm woozy.

Inkga leans forward. "They'll find him."

"You can't know that."

"No, but I have faith."

"Faith in what?" I scoff. "Daros? The only thing I have faith that he'll do is torture Nash." My voice comes out more anguished than I meant it to.

"No, Ryn. Faith that our men will find him and bring him home." Her voice is so soft. So believing.

But she's wrong.

There's nothing anyone can do.

"I should get some sleep."

"Of course." She stands and puts the chair back in place.

"Please let someone know if you need me. I'll be here in an instant."

I can't speak, only nod.

She gives me one last glance before leaving the room.

I blow out the candle by my bedside table and flop down onto the mattress. I force my eyes closed My body aches with exhaustion. I turn over and over, trying to find a comfortable position so I may fall asleep to talk to the First Queen.

I can't.

My thoughts stray to Nash. To what Daros is doing to him. Will Nash be tortured beyond repair despite my doing as they demanded?

Will he be killed?

Whatever happens, there's nothing I can do about it.

CHAPTER 21

I NEVER GET to sleep so I can talk to the First Queen. Never get any sort of comfort. Eventually, I get up and work out more. If I can't keep my mind together, I may as well keep my body active.

Inkga comes in with breakfast, but I can't bring myself to eat.

"You need your strength," she says.

I take a bite of bread and choke it down. Nash probably isn't getting any food at all.

Inkga picks out an outfit for me. I put it on without paying attention to what it is, but I make sure I have all my weapons on me.

She does something to my hair. I avoid my gaze in the mirror, not wanting to see the dark circles under my eyes.

She doesn't take the tray with her when she goes, like she usually does. Instead she says, "I'll leave this here, in case you decide you want something to eat. Also, Wilric has requested an audience."

"What does he want?"

She shrugs. "I'm uncertain. Is there anything else you need, My Lady?"

"Nothing. Thank you, Inkga. Please show Wilric into the sitting room."

She nods and is gone. I follow her to the sitting room, where I take a seat in my usual chair. I'd rather pace, but I don't want to appear more frantic than I already do.

What could Wilric want?

He comes in a moment later. "Your Majesty." He gives a deep bow.

"You may rise."

He stands in front of me.

"Take a seat," I say.

"I'm fine, my lady."

"Sit." If I have to, so does he.

He complies, picking the chair on my left. "I've come to talk to you about Nash."

I try not to flinch at the mention of his name. It's not that I can't hear it; it's that I can't hear it without thinking of what he's going through. "What about him?"

"I don't know if you are aware, but Nash and I are good friends."

I nod. I didn't know, but I'm not surprised.

"I can't stand to know my friend is captured and likely being tortured. I want your permission to take a team of men and go search for him."

"Why do you need my permission? Wouldn't Jaku let you go?"

"He probably would, but I'm afraid if I ask, he'll want me to stay on guard duty for you."

That might be a fair assessment. After all, my Head Advisor was kidnapped. What's to say they aren't coming for me next? "Why do you think you can find Nash when the rest of Jaku's men couldn't?"

"Because I know this town. It's huge, but I grew up patrolling it. I know how to find things here. I'm determined to find Nash. I just need your permission."

Finding Nash is like finding the mythical fila animal. Impossible. "You have it as long as you keep me updated."

The tightening around his eyes eases some. "Thank you, Your Majesty. I promise to let you know what we discover."

Another, stronger, thought comes to me. "No need. I will come with you."

He doesn't succeed in suppressing a cringe. "I'm certain your skills would be useful, but we can't risk you going out into public like that."

I thin my lips. I want to go. But he's right. Besides, I have duties to attend. "Fine."

He raises his eyebrows.

"Not what you expected?" I ask.

"Honestly, no, Your Majesty. From what I know, I expected you to fight me on this."

I sigh. "I want to, but I can't. I need to take care of the people. So you promise me you'll do everything you can to find him, and I'll do my part to keep everything else running smoothly."

"I promise, Your Highness."

"Get to it, then."

He nods and stands. "I will."

He leaves, giving me a moment alone. I slump back into my chair. Is this hope? I don't know.

After a moment, I go to the hall. I find Afet, Stird, Eldim, and two guards I don't recognize, both women. Jaku's upping the amount of guards on me.

To my servant that's waiting with them, I say, "Please bring me Jaku."

I spend the rest of the morning talking to Jaku and my ladies-in-waiting about everything, from Nash missing, to the state of the country, to the ladies'-in-waiting homes. Jem joins us, though she's not officially a lady-in-waiting any longer, and I prepare for this afternoon, when I will be addressing my people's concerns.

I dread it. They are going to be angry with me. I don't think I can handle their wrath at this moment, but I need to. If I'm going to change things on them, I have to show strength.

I spend lunchtime by myself. I need to eat, to keep my strength up, especially since I didn't eat much at breakfast. Again, I choke down some bread and protein, not tasting my food. Then it's time.

After Inkga arranges my hair around my crown, my guards and Jem follow me to the throne room. The last time I was here I was coronated. Now, I don't deserve it.

I should have never drunk the Mortum Tura. Then Nash would still be safe.

I sit on the throne. It's wrong. So wrong.

I'm a fraud.

I shouldn't be wearing this crown.

Guards surround me, like this place is filled with people, but there's no one. People will be admitted in small groups after they have been searched for weapons.

I still don't trust it, though. How can we check for everything? How do I know the guard checking them is on my side? I don't.

Nothing is safe.

But it's not my safety I'm worried about; it's Nash's.

I close my eyes and clench my jaw. Now is not the time to fall apart. I have to keep myself together, for the sake of my people.

Once I'm in control of myself, I say, "Let the first group in."

"Yes, Your Majesty." Jem stands at my side and does as I asked. She admits a group of people.

There are five of them—not many—and all wearing tattered clothes. Their faces are gaunt, their eyes haunted. There is a man, a woman, and what I assume would be their three children.

They bow. "Your Majesty." The man comes forward. "On behalf of my family, I would like to ask you why you made these changes to the tax law."

I freeze with my mouth half open. I don't know what to say. The truth would be best, but faced with him and the others, I flounder. I put Nash in the forefront of my thoughts. What he's going through. His sister begging me to save his life—save their family.

"I can offer you food. If you will visit the kitchens, I will make certain you have something to eat," I say.

"We don't want your food," the woman says. "We want what you promised us."

My throat threatens to close up. What have I done to my people? But what other choice do I have? I jump to my feet. "You will go to the kitchens, gather some food, and take it back to your family." I put a commanding voice into the demand, trying to ignore the pang in my chest. I motion to the closest servant. "See they have what I requested."

A guard ushers them back out of the room, with the servant hurrying after them.

The rest of the afternoon goes much the same, though the people don't always demand to know why I went back on my promise. They request food, despair heavy in their gazes.

As a Poruah family makes their way out, a Kurah man, richly dressed in purple robes, sneers at them. I'm making this divide among my people worse. Is this what Nash would want? Is it even helping him? It's been a day. Why hasn't Daros returned him?

CHAPTER 22

DESPITE IT BEING sometime in the middle of the night and desperately wanting to talk to the First Queen, I can't sleep. The harder I try, the more awake I feel.

I toss and turn. Turn and toss. Until I can't stand it anymore.

I fling myself out of bed and dress in black pants and a black shirt. I stash my weapons on me. The question is do I go look for Nash by myself, or do I take someone? Whatever the case may be, there's a sense of urgency. The longer Daros has him, the less confident I feel I'll ever see him again.

Preferably, I'd go by myself, but Nash would be upset if I did so. I have to take someone. Which means I'll end up taking a lot of someones.

Not what I want, but if it helps find Nash...

I stalk to my sitting room and open the door. The guards and a servant jump. Apparently, they weren't expecting me.

"Does anyone know if Wilric is back?" I ask.

"He is," Afet says. "He got back about an hour ago, Your Majesty. He said if we saw you before he did, to tell you he's found nothing so far."

Drat and double drat.

If he hadn't just gotten back, I'd take him with me, but he's going to need his sleep. I'll go with what I have. I look my guards over. They're wearing their uniforms. "I need all of you to go change into something black."

"We can't leave you alone, Your Majesty," Eldim says.

"Then go one at a time. Better yet, I'll come with you." I look at the servant. "Please stay here. I will be back before sunup."

He looks like he wants to protest, but all he does is bow. "Yes, Your Majesty."

Stird leads the way while Eldim, Afet, and a familiar guard whose name I don't know, follow me. We go through the palace halls, down a secret hallway, and come out by the barracks, next to the one Nash was staying in.

My gut feels as if it's been punched.

I hurry past, trying to ignore the feeling, but it won't go away. It kicks at me, making my stomach sore.

I wait outside the guards' building with the group, while they each take a turn changing so as not to leave me alone.

Once they're all in black, Afet says, "If I may inquire, Your Majesty, what are we doing?"

"Looking for Nash."

They all nod, like this is what they expected. I wait for someone to protest, but none of them do. We make our way to the portcullis, where we're stopped by a guard. I give him a look, and he bows. "Your Majesty, forgive me. I didn't expect to see you out at this hour. How may we be of service?"

"I am going to go into the city. Let us pass, and then let us back in when I return."

He looks to one side, then the other. "I... um..."

"You won't fight me on this. You won't get Jaku. You will let us through." I put a hand on my dagger.

"Yes, Your Majesty." He bows again.

I shake my head, still not used to such deference. It's a little hard to handle. But he does his job. He tells another guard to have the portcullis lifted, and soon we are out into the city. The park area is lit with torches, bringing a flickering beauty to the area.

Where do we search first? "Let's see if I missed anything at Daros's house."

"I'm not sure we brought enough guards to protect you," the female guard says.

I narrow my eyes. "What's your name?"

"Julina, Your Majesty."

She has pretty brown hair and dazzling green eyes. None of that will help us in a fight, though.

"Don't you trust your abilities?" I ask.

"I do. Only—forgive me, but—you are the queen." She says the last word in a whisper, though there's no one around the palace grounds this time of night. "I'm worried about what would happen if someone got wind of this. Last time, you drew a huge crowd. This time, if that happens…"

They might maul me, after what I did to their taxes.

Is this want Daros wanted? To turn the people against me? Why not try to kill me and be done with it? What does he have to gain from this plan? Now's not the time to worry over it.

"Either you trust your abilities, or you can leave us now. I am fine doing this on my own." I don't need their help.

She straightens. "I'm coming."

I should have tested them before bringing them out, but there was no time.

I move at an almost run, grateful there are no people out to stall me. As we go through the streets, it's hard not to remember other times I've been out like this. Times I was sent to kill.

I shiver.

I can't get lost in regrets. I have to keep going.

Several minutes later, we arrive at Daros's. It's dark. Every house around here is, with everyone gone off to bed some time ago.

It'd be nice to do the same.

I enter the house without knocking. If someone is here, I don't want them aware of our presence. I find several candle holders in the first room, light them, and pass them out.

I tiptoe through the house, my guards close by and noisier than I want. Other than that, it's eerily silent. So much so, I'm almost grateful for my guards' noise.

Each room is barer than the last, like someone came through and took what they wanted from the house. Looters? My guess is Daros. I can't see him allowing looters to take what belongs to him. But I have been wrong before.

When we get to the office, I hesitate. No one is inside, but the memories flood me. I often came to his office in the middle of the night after finishing a job, hating myself even as he told me *well done*. The kindest words I ever got out of him.

He'd pour a glass of wine and celebrate while I watched. Sick. Hurting. Lonely. It's not something I want to relive now any more than I wanted to live it then.

I shove the thoughts away as I scour the room for any sign of him. Nothing is different from the last time I was here, except maybe the chill in the air.

I move into the secret room. Nothing here. Not even the dead body and torture devices. The body was properly taken care of, but what happened to the torture devices?

A sickening thought hits me.

He took them to use them on Nash.

The world sways. I brace myself against the nearest wall.

"Your Majesty?" A faint whisper yet frantic in tone. "Are you all right? What happened?"

I have to pull myself together. I can't help Nash if I'm wobbly at the thought of those devices. I knew what they were doing to him.

I shouldn't have come here.

Shouldn't have reminded myself of what Daros is capable of.

"Has anyone been watching this house?" I hope against hope

that someone has. That someone saw something but didn't think to report it.

My guards share gazes. Finally, Afet says, "I don't believe a watch was set up, Your Highness."

I punch the wall. My knuckles barely feel the sting, but my heart aches from it.

"Let's go," I say. "There's nothing for us here."

Tight-lipped and pale, the escorts follow me out.

Once we're back in the open, Stird asks, "Where to now?"

Good question. I haven't the faintest idea. If Daros had left a clue behind... Of course, he's much too smart for that. If he left anything behind, it'd be because he wanted us to see it.

He wanted me to know those torture devices went missing.

My head swims.

I can't do this.

But I have to.

"We'll check out the warehouse district by the market." It's not an area I frequented often, but it seems like a good place to hide someone. Lots of people are going in and out all the time, but there are empty buildings too.

Eldim leads the way. As much as I feel like I could be doing this on my own, I'm grateful for their support. If they weren't here, I might curl up in a ball and never unwind.

At first, the streets remain quiet, people in the richer districts having gone to bed some time ago. As we near the warehouse section, first there's one person on the streets, then a few. I keep my focus on our destination, pretending I belong on the streets as much as I did months ago.

There's more to the warehouses than I remember. So many places to hide Nash, and we don't even know if he's here.

I move to the closest warehouse and put my ear to the door. Nothing. I try the handle. Locked. No problem. I slip out my lock-picking tools and have it unlocked within a minute. I nod for the others to go inside. A couple do, and the rest follow me in.

It's dark inside. I wait for my eyes to adjust. There are wooden crates with something in them. It smells of oil, grease, and fish. I switch to breathing through my mouth. We pick our way through aisles of boxes, finding nothing in the big warehouse except more boxes. They aren't big enough to hide a human the size of Nash, even if Daros's men tried to squeeze him in as a form a torture.

We go through several more buildings with more of the same. Only the smell is different. I'm beginning to feel it's a hopeless task. I knew Daros wouldn't make it easy, but I had to try.

Though it's still dark out, more people are showing up. Work down here must start early. A few watch us with careful eyes, but most ignore us.

"What now?" Stird asks.

"We continue searching." Though we can't hold out much longer with this many people about.

"What about the workers?" Afet keeps an eye on the ones closest to us.

"I am who I am," I say. "I can go wherever I want." It had better be true. I don't want to push my luck, but I do want to find him.

We approach the next unsearched warehouse. It's smaller than the others, but could easily hold a mountain of food. We'll search this last one, and then head back to the palace for the night. Morning is nearing.

We slip inside. It has a dusty scent, but nothing stronger, though crates are stacked around. We wind our way through the aisles but there are only crates. There's nothing here to lead us to Nash.

This search was a waste.

I want to throw my dagger in frustration, but refrain.

Afet leads us out of the warehouse onto the streets. It's lighter outside—not by a lot, but enough that I can see a little better. We have to return to the palace so they don't worry about me.

"Hey," a male voice rings out. "What do you think you were doing in my warehouse?"

Trouble.

"We're from the palace, on official duty," Afet says. "We're looking for something."

The man sneers. "From the palace, huh? I don't think you have a right to any of my stuff. Jop, get over here."

Another man approaches. He has enough muscles to rival any of my guards. Of course, my guards are trained, and odds are, this man isn't.

"These people are from the palace. Been snooping around my stuff," the first man tells Jop.

Jop scowls at us. "You aren't allowed in here. Go back and tell your queen she's taken everything from us. There's nothing left for her here."

Maybe that's why the last warehouse had no distinctive smell —all the crates were empty. It's enough to make me tense. I didn't want to take everything from them. If I could just find Nash, I'd change things back to how they were.

A chilling thought hits me.

Why would they give him back if they know I will return everything to the way it should be?

They'll keep him alive until he's of no more use to them, then kill him.

I sway.

"We'll be getting out of your way." Stird takes a step back.

"I don't think so," Jop says. "Someone needs to pay for what your queen has done."

"Don't you think we agree with you?" I say coming to my senses. I have to get us out of this situation before I fall apart. "We weren't the ones to play with your taxes. It's that queen."

He eyes me like he's trying to decide if he should believe me or not.

"It's true," Julina says. "We hate what she's done as much as you do."

"Then why are you down here, doing her business?"

"Because we still have to do our jobs, like you have to do yours." She is steady. Calm.

I can't stand here, arguing. "Look. We have to go, but the queen is going to be listening to grievances from the people again today. You should go to the castle and complain about what she's done."

"I know something that would send her a better message." Jop grins like he won something.

Others are moving closer, surrounding us. My fingers itch to grab my daggers, but I don't just yet. No sense starting a fight if there's a way to avoid it.

"We don't want any trouble," I say. "Please go see the queen later today, and you can discuss this with her."

"Too bad we want trouble." Jop pulls out a sword. All around we hear the faint scratch of blades being drawn.

I grit my teeth. I don't want to hurt any of my people, but neither can I let them hurt me or my escorts.

"Please," Afet says. "We just want to leave peacefully."

"Not happening."

"Fine. But don't say we didn't give you a chance to run away." I throw my daggers before they know what's coming to them. One lands in Jop's right arm, and the other in the first man's right bicep. They both drop their swords with curses.

"Don't stand there," Jop screams. "Get them."

"Try not to hurt them too badly," I call out.

It's not a fair fight, by a long shot. The only thing that gives the people fighting against me a chance is that we're not trying to hurt them if possible, but we're also not putting ourselves in danger; we're trying to work our way out of here.

The scent of fresh blood fills the air. I want to gag, but instead, keep my weapons at the ready. A man comes barreling at me. I raise my weapons, but Julina steps in front of me, blocking his access to me. All around me, my guards are fighting, their swords flashing but not injuring.

I step toward the street we need to use to get out of here, and the others follow suit even as they continue their fight. The clang of metal and cursing sounds through the street. If we don't hurry, we're going to attract more attention to ourselves, which is the last thing we need.

If only there was a way to knock them out, but my poisons kill; they don't just simply render the subject unconscious. My blades do the same. I'll have to choke out our attackers or knock them unconscious.

The men we're brawling against are tenacious, banging their weapons as hard as they can against my soldiers' blades. Despite that, their rebuttals are weakening. Their faces grow desperate.

"We won't hurt you if you give up now," I call out.

Instead of having the effect I want my words to, they growl, bringing new life to the fray. I should keep my mouth shut.

We work our way back, me trying to get in, to help my guards fight, and them blocking me even as they struggle to get people off.

I'm making this worse on them than if I wasn't trying to help them.

I helplessly continue to inch back toward the street as they fight and move as a group. My guards are well-trained, aiming their blades toward limbs but not hacking them off—barely nicking them, but doing enough damage that the men are hesitant.

A hiss sounds behind me. I turn to find Julina punching a man. The man goes down.

"Are you all right?" I ask her.

"Just a scratch. Come on. Let's go while there's an opening."

I follow after her, the other guards bringing up the rear. The men they were fighting cheer behind us like they won the clash. That they don't understand how much my soldiers were holding back is for the best.

"Any other injuries besides Julina?" I ask, once we're several blocks away and have slowed to a fast walk.

No one replies. Either they're not hurt, or they don't want to admit to it.

"Julina, show me your injury," I say.

"I'm fine."

"Show me." I use my voice that means business.

She grunts but turns toward me and rolls up the sleeve of her shirt. There, on her lower bicep, is a deep cut.

"You'll need stitches," I say, as I cut part of the bottom of my shirt. I wrap the wound to slow the bleeding and tie it off, careful not to make contact with her skin.

She gives me a look I don't understand.

"Thank you," she says.

Is that what that look is? Gratitude? Maybe a little awe mixed in? I turn away. We have a long way before we make it back to the palace.

CHAPTER 23

WE SHOW up to the open portcullis, a bedraggled group. There are several more guards than usual, along with Jaku.

I glare at the guard who lets us in.

"Don't blame him," Jaku says. "I went looking for you last night and couldn't find you. What were you doing going out without telling me?"

I want to use my old excuse of *I am the queen* but it feels trite. Besides, Jaku has been nothing but helpful. Something dawns on me. "Were you coming to find me because you have news?"

He forms a thin line with his lips as he shakes his head. "I'm afraid there's no news. I was checking in on you, to make sure everything was all right. I'm being extra cautious, with what's happened."

"At least there hasn't been an attack on my life." There have only been a couple since the ball. Nothing major that I'm aware of.

"Don't jinx it."

I head toward the palace in the growing sunlight as the men lower the portcullis. "Superstitious?"

"Not in the least, but where you're life is concerned, we can't be too careful."

"Have there been queens that didn't get attacks on their lives?"

"Some have less. That's why some live longer than others. Of course, that also tends to make us complacent."

Will I ever become complacent? I would say *no*, but that's the thing about it. You never realize it's happening.

"You should get some rest," Jaku says.

He doesn't know how desperately I need it. To talk to the First Queen. "Later. I promised I would meet with the people today."

"The same people you threw daggers at, Your Highness?" Julina's voice is steady.

I give her a sideways glance. "Yes, those people."

"You threw daggers at them?" Jaku sounds anything but steady.

"In all fairness, they attacked her first," Julina says.

"They what?" By the way he's squeezing his eyes shut tight, he's barely holding back his anger.

I stride up the palace steps, not missing a beat. "They attacked, but we took care of them. There will likely be some repercussions for the palace. I wish we could send peace and food their way, but I'm afraid it would only lead to more attacks."

"I'll put extra guards on the front gate. Are you certain you want to hold court this afternoon?"

"I need to. The people are angry at me enough. If I don't listen to them, how am I ever going to earn their trust back?" Like those people at the throne room that I previously didn't really listen to, instead sending them home with food. It's not that I don't want to listen, it's that I don't know what to say. I can't tell them what's happening.

It's going to be a hard road. One I'd rather take with Nash back at my side. I sweep his name away, trying to pretend it never crossed my thoughts.

If he's not back, maybe I should revert the taxes. There's no sense keeping them like this if Daros isn't going to fulfill his end of the bargain. The thought of telling Nash's family I've given up haunts me. I can't do that to them.

We enter the palace and turn through the halls instead of going straight to the chalice room as I did that fateful day.

"Is there anything else you need me doing today?" Jaku asks.

"Make certain that the people are properly searched before they come and see me. I don't want any surprises. And someone see that Julina gets stitched up." Not that I couldn't handle any surprises, but like earlier, they won't thank me for leaving them bleeding.

"Yes, Your Majesty."

Several minutes later, when we reach my rooms, he bows. "If you will excuse me, Your Highness, there are some things I need to take care of."

I wave him away as I step into my sitting room. Inkga is here, twisting her hands together so hard they're turning red. I excuse my guards.

"Are you all right?" I ask her.

She drops her hands to her sides. "I've been worried about you, my lady."

"I'm here now. Sorry to leave you without a word."

"You're the queen. You don't have to leave word."

"I should have done it anyway." Because, despite my reservations, I care for her as a friend, and I don't want to her to worry about me.

"I'll get breakfast if you're ready," she says as if compromising.

I nod for her to do so and move to my bedroom. While she's away, I pick out a dress. Something more formal than I care for—stately, but not overdone—but that will hopefully show the people how serious I am about addressing their concerns, even if I can't fix them all right now. It's all I can give them without reverting the law. I decide on a simple purple dress with a slash through the skirt, revealing white fabric beneath. It's not Poruah clothing, but neither is it Kurah.

Mostly though, I want to get back out there and look for Nash. There's no sense worrying about it with so much to do. Besides,

I'm not sure I was doing any good out there, anyway. It's not like I know where Daros stashed him. Daros trusted me with so little.

There's a knock, and Inkga comes in with a breakfast tray. I sit down at my vanity to eat. Though it's like sand in my mouth, my body is grateful for the sustenance.

"Would you like a bath and a trip to the queen's spring?"

"Just a bath, please." I have no wish to relive the memory of the spring I almost let myself be killed in.

"I'll have one sent for right away."

She leaves the room and comes back a moment later. She idly chats while I eat my breakfast. At one point, the chatter would have bothered me, but now I find it soothing.

"Is this the dress you picked out to wear for the day?" she asks.

"It is." I shove my mostly empty tray away. I wasn't hungry but needed the sustenance. "I was hoping for something that looked a little queenlier, for the people to see me in."

"That is a good choice."

There's another knock. She answers it, and I spend the rest of the morning in a flurry of activity, getting ready. Once I'm bathed and dressed in the deep-purple outfit, Inkga helps me with my hair that's grown a little longer. When it's done, she brings me my crown from the royal treasury, and I place it on my head.

"Do I look like I could face a crowd of angry people?" I ask.

"You do, and you'll do fine."

I sigh. "I wish I didn't have to give into someone else's demands in order to keep Nash alive."

"I know. You'll find him, and then you can make everything right."

I have the strangest urge to hug her, but I refuse to bring the law down on her head, even if it means feeling lonely.

I make my way to the throne room, a new group of guards accompanying me. The ones from last night should be off, getting some rest. I could too, but I must do what little I can to calm my people.

Once I'm seated on the throne, I take a steadying breath. Bring on more complaints about me. I'm ready to handle them.

The day starts off much like yesterday. The complaints are many, and mostly to do with my tax changes. There's not much I can do for them, though I offer food and clothing where I can. If I have to take their money, then I can at least spend it on helping them however I can.

Little is seen from the Kurah class, but the Poruah and Medi class abound. It's all the same, hurting my chest with each new person.

Until a woman, dressed in a simple green skirt and white blouse with a kind face but with brown eyes that are full of anger, enters. She stands straight, like she has a backbone of iron.

"How can I help you?" I ask.

"Your Majesty." Her curtsy can barely be considered that. "I have a complaint against your guards. They are beating people. Injuring them so severely they can't work." That doesn't sound like my guards or any other complaint I've heard, but maybe there's more going on that I'm not aware of. A problem I can finally fix. "My husband had a dagger thrown into his shoulder. He'll be out of work for months, if he can ever return."

A sick feeling settles in my gut. "Is he with you?"

"He didn't want to come in."

"I'd like to meet him anyway, if you would please bring him."

A guard leaves the room and returns moments later with a familiar face.

One of the men I daggered. As he approaches, recognition etches his features. "You did this to me," he says.

"You will not address Her Majesty this way," the guard says, blocking the man from coming at me.

"No, he's right." Guilt makes my words bitter. "I did harm him." I turn my attention to the man. "Your group attacked me and my guards. We were searching for someone who is being hurt. We weren't doing anything bad to your area when we were recognized and attacked. We protected ourselves."

He spits on the gleaming wooden floor. "You were taking whatever you wanted from us, and you know it."

"I'm truly sorry for how this played out. I will send you home with several months' pay and food to see your family through." I motion for a servant.

"I don't want your stuff," the man growls.

His wife takes him by his uninjured upper arm. "We could use that money."

"I don't want anything that comes from her."

He turns and storms out of the throne room, stomping his boots. The wife gives me a pleading look before following him.

"See that they are given what I promised," I tell the servant. "Do your best to get the wife to accept it."

"Yes, Your Highness."

As the servant scurries from the room, my heart is tight with pain. What am I doing to my people?

CHAPTER 24

I PACE a frantic path across my room. There's nothing on my mind except Nash. Where is he? What's happening to him? What can I do to help? The thoughts swirl over and over, making it hard to think.

There's a knock, and I rush to open it. Wilric stands before me. I hurry him in. "Any news?"

He shakes his head, mouth set in a grim line. "Nothing out of the ordinary. Everything seems to be as it should. The people we're interviewing know nothing. The places we search are coming up empty."

"What about Daros's known associates? Did anything come from the list I gave you?"

"We found Merloch, but he insisted he knows nothing about Daros's current whereabouts."

That can't be. "He must know what's going on. Give us a small clue. Anything."

"He said he hasn't seen Daros in several years. And before you ask, yes, I checked out his story. He seems to be clean lately. Owns a tavern and does honest work. If he's had any contact with Daros, it's well-hidden."

"Nash is suffering somewhere. This isn't good enough."

"I agree completely, but we're doing what we can."

I slouch. "He has to be somewhere."

"He is. We just have to find out where." He looks me head on. "We'll find him. It's a big city, and it's going to take some time, but we'll find him."

"Before they destroy him?" The words are out, though I should have stopped them.

"It's going to be all right." The words are soothing, but with nothing to go on, I can't believe him.

"You don't know that. No one does." I shouldn't say such things. I should be working on finding solutions, but I'm at a loss as to what move should be made next.

He sighs. "Perhaps you're right, but I have hope that everything is going to turn out fine."

"I don't know what it means to hope." Nothing in my life has led me to do so. That's not changing now since Nash has been captured by the worst person alive.

Wilric takes a step closer, bending his head down. "It means a lot of things, but all you have to focus on is that I will get Nash back."

"I can't believe that, as much as I want to."

"Then I'll hope enough for the both of us."

Some of the tumultuous noise in my chest settles down. "Do you mean that?"

"I do."

"I can see why Nash counted you as a friend."

He almost smiles, but it's tainted with the devastation in his gaze. "Thank you, my lady."

"How long have you known Nash?" I ask.

"Almost my whole life. My family moved near his when I was six. I've been friends with him ever since."

Wilric has much more of a claim on Nash than I do. It doesn't stop me from worrying or caring. If anything, it gives me a stronger reason to bring Nash home.

"Now if you'll excuse me, I need to get some rest so I can have an early start in the morning."

"Of course." I don't want him here, talking to me, if it's going to cut into the time he could be searching for Nash. "Please make sure you take whatever resources you need to find him."

"I will." He bows. "I'll update you again as soon as I can, Your Majesty."

He leaves the room. I almost start pacing again, but it won't help me find Nash any faster.

But there is something I can do that will mean a lot to Nash's family.

I send a servant for Pina. Only a few minutes later, she arrives. "How can I help you, Your Majesty?"

"I want you to take down a note for me and deliver it to Nash's family. Make sure you bring a couple guards with you. The city is a dangerous place for anyone associated with the palace these days."

She waves away my concern. "I'll take some guards then, and everything will be fine." She pulls out a quill, ink, and paper from a drawer in my low table. "What do you want the note to say?"

I give her a quick overview of Wilric's report. It's not the news I want to send, but I want to keep them as up to date as I can.

Once the note is written and Pina sent on her way, cloaked and with an armed escort, I start exercising. My thoughts should be with my people and how I can make it up to them—how I can fix what I broke. Instead, I'm struggling to come to terms with the fact that Nash is in Daros's hands.

CHAPTER 25

HOURS AND HOURS and hours later, I'm exhausted. I'm trained to go with little sleep, but this is ridiculous. I've rested for a few snippets here and there, but I keep jostling awake with fear that something's happened to Nash. And I'm exhausted.

I finish my supper, eyes closing.

"I think you should go to bed, Your Majesty," Inkga says.

"Maybe you're right." And maybe tonight I'll be able to sleep for long enough to talk to the First Queen.

I climb into bed, and Inkga takes away my tray.

"Please call me if you need anything," she says. "Anything at all."

"And I'll let you know if I decide to go out looking for him again." I slur my words, but I can't seem to help it.

"That would be appreciated. Goodnight, Your Majesty." Her voice is soft. Distant.

I find the daggers under my pillow and let my hand rest on them. With my other hand, I grab hold of the doll the sweet girl gave me and hold it close.

The colors of the sunset merge together in a beautiful array. "You have had a hard few days," *the First Queen says.*

"I'm so glad to be able to talk to you. I need your help." My voice is desperate. At least she's the only one who can hear it.

"Before you ask—no. I can't use magic to find Nash Zorris."

I slump down into a sitting position. "Why not?"

"Because magic isn't that easy. It has to be imbued into an object to work. It takes time and patience. More skill than you have."

"But I need it. I'll do anything to get it."

She lifts an eyebrow. "Anything?"

I think before I speak. Would I do anything? I've already gone further than I should have. "I just want him back. Want him safe."

"I know."

"You can't know." I'm being rude, but I don't care. "You never lived through what I did. You don't understand what they're doing to Nash."

She sits back against the bright oranges and reds. "It's true. I don't know. I'm afraid you keep those memories locked up tight, though we've talked about it. You won't let me understand."

I turn away. "It's too much for anyone to deal with."

"I can't imagine what you went through to make you feel that way."

I release a breath in a huff and turn back around. "What do I do about Nash?"

"You don't want to hear my opinion."

"I know, but I need to."

She stares at me a moment. "You know taking care of a country is bigger than one person. One man."

I cringe. "I know. But I can't leave him to his fate." My voice is small.

"You need to think of the greater good."

I don't reply. What's the use?

"I know you care deeply for Nash."

I do. More than I thought. I close my eyes, willing away the tears building.

"You need to think about what's most important."

"What do you mean?"

"Exactly what I said."

This is getting me nowhere, or maybe nowhere I want to go. "You said I needed more skill to use magic, how do I get those skills?"

She purses her lips. "It's complicated. Time, patience, practice, and I'm afraid you only have the practice part down."

She's right. I don't have time or patience, even if I do know how to practice. It's not good enough, though. I need to do something, anything, to get me closer to finding Nash. "You know magic. Teach me."

"It's not that simple. I wish it was, but it's not something I can cover in the short amount of time as a dream. It takes years and years of practice to have any small result."

"That's not good enough." My words are harsh.

"That may be, but it's what I can give you."

"You're not giving me anything. You're no help at all." I grit my teeth.

She frowns, creases marring her smooth features.

I rub my head. "I'm sorry. I didn't mean it."

"It's all right. You're under a great deal of pressure."

"It's not all right. I want nothing to do with being like Daros, yet here I am losing my temper and raging at you like he would. I have to do better."

"We all have to do better, but it takes time. Change doesn't happen overnight. It's hard work that comes with practice."

There's that practice word again. I want to curse it. Little good it does me now when I have no time for it. "Don't you have anything that can help now?"

"I'm sorry."

I feel myself waking. Not yet. I'm not ready to go; I still need to talk to her.

But before she answers, I wake.

CHAPTER 26

WELL INTO THE MORNING, I'm stewing over the First Queen's words, though it does me no good.

I meet with several groups.

Timit is in the long line of people who want my attention. "I have papers for you to sign."

"And what are they about?" I stop myself from rubbing my eyes. Despite getting some sleep last night, I'm still worn to the bone.

"They are for funding the new section of the palace."

That wakes me right up. "Who's building that?"

"You are, Your Majesty. Every queen does."

I dismiss him with a wave of my hand. "There's not to be such waste while I am queen. What I want from you is a report on how we can handle lower taxes for the Poruah."

"But, Your Highness, you just raised them."

"Pretend I didn't. I want to know how we can make it work on a limited budget."

He purses his meaty lips. "I put together that report before you went back on the changes, but may I respectfully suggest that you keep the taxes as they are? There will have to be too many cutbacks if we lose the income from so many."

"They are poor enough to begin with. We don't need to be taking more from them." I hold out my hand. "Give me the report."

With a scowl, he places a thin stack of papers in my hands. I scan them over several minutes, an uncomfortable relief filling me. This is more workable than I thought, but I have no plans to change it soon. I need Nash safe first. For his family. For Wilric.

For me, if I'm honest with myself.

I shove the thoughts away. "It looks like we could lower the taxes on the Poruah some as well, and still have plenty of money in the treasury."

Timit splutters. "What do you expect us to live on?"

"You are getting far more gold than one person needs." Which was hidden well within the many documents. "I suggest you stop buying so many expensive things and live more simply."

He stands. "This is an outrage." Spittle goes flying. Thankfully, it all misses me. "I cannot agree with any such changes and will be vehemently against anything you do that undermines the government's ability to rule."

"According to this report you yourself made, with a little bit of cutting back, we'll be fine," I say. "What about the mines? Did you find out anything about them?"

"They're privately held by different Kurah. The government doesn't own any and can't benefit from them."

Something to think about. "Very well. Now, if you will excuse me, I have others I need to see."

He opens and closes his mouth before he storms from the room.

I sink back into my chair, rubbing my temples. Living on lower taxes is possible but not in line with keeping Nash alive.

And why haven't I heard anything? What is Daros doing with him?

To distract myself, I shuffle through the other paperwork on my lap, putting the unhelpful pages on the low table in front of me and making another pile of the ones that may help. There has to be some type of loophole—some way I can fund the Poruah and Medi classes without changing taxes.

The words start to blur together when there's a knock. "Come in."

Wilric enters and stands before me.

"How are things? Do you have any news?" I ask.

"I'm so sorry, Your Majesty. We are getting a lot of the city searched, but we have found no sign of him so far. I promise you we will, though. I won't allow us to fail."

I close my eyes, trying to control my emotions, not opening them again until I've gotten a hold of myself.

"Is there anything else we should know?" he asks. "Any more places you've thought of? People we haven't heard of that we should check out?"

I shake my head. It would be good if there was something, but there's nothing more than what I've told them previously. I clench my teeth together to stop from falling apart.

He kneels down before me, looking up at me. "I will find him."

"And if you don't?"

"That's not an option."

I like him more than ever. "One more thing—where does Nash's family live?"

He gives me directions, stands, and with a bow says, "If you'll excuse me now, I'll get back to my search."

"Thank you."

He leaves, and I want to go with him, but Jaku would be upset with me if I did. That, and I have duties here. More things to oversee. A people to take care of, which I've been doing a terrible job at. There is something I am determined to do, though. I need to see his family in person.

I go into my room and find a dress that will fit in with the general populace. Something ordinary with few frills. Thanks to Inkga, it's there along with other fantastic options and not just fancy things. I grab the cloak Nash gave me the first time I went out into town with him. I finger the brown fabric, feeling its coarse material. I want to sit down and cry with it.

But I won't.

I will be strong.

I throw it on and head to the door. Outside, Eldim, Julina, and two guards whose names I don't know are waiting for me.

I tell my servant, "Fetch Jaku for me." I'd better tell him what I have planned this time. No sense worrying him needlessly.

She hurries down the hall, and I wait with my guards, not bothering to go back in my room. They watch me out of the corner of their eyes but no one says anything.

A few minutes later, the servant returns with Jaku at her side.

He bows, and after I tell him to rise, says, "You called for me."

"Yes. I'm taking my guards and going to Nash's family. They need to hear from their queen what is being done to help their son."

"I'm not sure that's wise, Your Majesty. We don't know who might recognize you and what type of trouble it might stir up."

"I'll keep my head covered. Anyway, I'm going."

He rubs his eyes with his hand. "Fine, but let me go with you."

"I'm sure you have other duties you need to attend to."

"My first duty is to keeping you safe. That's what I'm going to do."

I peer at him. "Very well. But we're leaving within the next half hour. You five need to change into something that will help you blend into the crowd."

I can't believe it takes five people for me to go from one place to another. It's silly. I could take them all on myself and come out alive.

We go to the barracks and wait while they change one at a time. Soon, we are out of the gates and headed into town, following the directions I got from Wilric. It's a twisting, long way.

"We should have taken horses," I say.

"Except they would have made us stand out more," Jaku says."

He's right. There's no one else riding out here. I wonder why, and then it comes to me.

Only the richest can afford such luxuries.

And I've made the income divide worse.

I steel myself against such thoughts. I can't have them bringing me down at a time like this. Maybe tonight, when I'm trying to go to sleep, they can haunt me. Now I need my wits about me.

The farther we go from the palace, the closer together the houses grow. We move to an area that is neither poor, nor rich. A lower-middle class. The houses are well taken care of, but small. The streets are fairly clean and clear, but some of the cobblestones are missing. The fences around the houses are similar—nice, but a little faded, and with the occasional piece of wood missing.

We arrive at a quaint little house. It's got charm, with flowers at the windows and more in a pot at the doorstep. The bricks are mostly fine, but there are a few cracks here and there—nothing that would harm the structure, but something that should have been fixed before now.

I knock while my guards cover my back and sides. It only takes a moment for the door to open.

Belta, Nash's oldest sister, has a frown on her face and red eyes that widen when she sees me. "Your Majesty," she curtseys and I hurry her up. "Please, come in."

I enter, conscious that I'm walking in the same place Nash grew up in. These halls were his. This living room with the sofa and chairs made of wood have all been used by him. The floor is covered with worn rugs. Another sign they don't have enough money, despite my increasing Nash's pay with his new position and paying his sisters for their help with the ball.

"If you'll excuse me, I'll go get my mother." Belta curtseys and hurries from the room.

There aren't enough seats for all five of us plus their mom and sisters, so I remain standing.

There's a shuffle of movement in the hallway, and moments later, Slipa hurries out into the room.

Her eyes are clear, and her mouth turns up in a smile at the sight of me. That doesn't help the ache in my heart at seeing her.

"Your Majesty." She curtseys. "Have you found him? Please, sit."

I reluctantly take a seat. I take the nearest wooden chair. My guards quickly spread throughout the room, with Eldim staying close by and Jaku at the window.

Slipa sits on the couch, and Belta and Lanay come in the room to take a seat beside her.

"I wish I was here for pleasure. Wish I had better news."

Slipa's smile falls. "Is he... dead?"

"No, no. Nothing like that." Not to my knowledge.

She sighs. "We know you're doing the best you can."

But am I? I only went out to look once. It wasn't enough. "I wanted to let you know we are still looking. I have many guards out there searching for him. Plus one of my personal guards, Wilric, you may know, is leading a team of men. He promised he will find him."

"I know he will." Her voice cracks. "Sorry." A tear escapes. "Nash is just my baby, you know?"

I don't, but I nod.

Belta puts an arm around her mother, her face scrunching with pain.

"If I may... You are welcome to come live at the palace. I'd be able to keep you more up to date there," I say.

Slipa shakes her head. "What if he were to get free and come home, and not find us here? No. Your notes have been keeping us informed well enough. I want to stay at home. Where the memories are."

I want to argue with her, but Nash did think the palace was a dangerous place to live. Besides, she's right; none of her memories with him are there. They're all treasured here. "Tell me more about Nash."

Slipa's chin shakes, but Lanay speaks up. "He was—is—the best brother. I remember, when I was still a little girl, he would put me on his shoulders, and we would go to the market together. We'd look at all the fine things, and he'd promise to buy me something, when he could afford it. I never thought he'd be able to get me any of the baubles I wanted, but one day, after he'd been a soldier for some years, he came home with this."

She holds out her arm and on her wrist is a gorgeous bracelet. On a soldier's pay, it must have taken years to save up for. The blue stones are so bright and pretty and look smooth. I want to run my fingers across them but don't dare get that close to touching her.

"He got Belta one just like it, too," Lanay continues. "I don't know how much it cost, but it told me my brother always kept me and my sister in mind. That he wanted to make sure we knew we were loved." Her voice cracks on that last word, and I feel like I've stepped into something more personal than I should have.

We talk for a while more. The more I hear about him, the more determined I become to save him. Daros has him out there somewhere and is mocking me with his capture, but it won't last. I will find him, and I will rescue him.

CHAPTER 27

"WELCOME BACK, YOUR MAJESTY." Inkga's face is far too white.

"What's wrong?" I ask.

"Who said anything was wrong?" Her smile is tight.

"Your face. I can tell."

Her expression falls. "I was hoping you'd get a good night's sleep before you got the news. Or at least a good meal in you."

"Tell me." I hate to be harsh to her; I consider her a good friend. But I have to know what's going on.

"You received another note while you were away." She holds out a sealed envelope.

I take it from her and break the seal.

YOU WILL GET RID of your lady in waiting and appoint Tido Sauvers as your new Head Advisor. Do this, or Nash will pay.

THE NOTE FLUTTERS to the ground.

What is Daros going to do to Nash now? What is wrong with Jem? Who is Tido Sauvers, and why does Daros want him in as

Head Advisor? Why won't he let me be? Why won't he return Nash?

Too many questions, and I fear I know the answer. He's using me. Manipulating me like Ranen planned on doing with Jem.

I bend down and pick up the note. It's flown open. I hand it to Inkga. "Read it if you want. It doesn't matter."

I collapse into the closest chair. Are they going to control me the rest of my life? How can I allow this? It's unthinkable.

As is letting Nash suffer.

"Are you going to follow through with it?" Inkga asks.

"I don't know. Part of me wants to refuse. To throw it in their faces. But I don't know how I can dare."

"I don't know either. I wish I could be more helpful to you."

"Bring me Jem and Jaku. Also, do you know where this letter came from?"

"It was found in your room. On your pillow."

I feel the blood drain from my head. How did they get so close to me? I'd taken all my guards with me, but still, someone should have heard or seen something.

"Bring in my guards," I say.

Inkga hurries from the room. I don't know what to do. I look out the window, wishing none of this ever happened and Nash was still here. That I never let Daros live.

I've wished it all too many times, and yet reality doesn't change. Wishing does no good.

What do you think I should do? I silently ask the First Queen.

I know what she would say. That I need to do what's best for the people. I need to think of others before I think of Nash. I can't put him before the country. My country.

The council will probably say the same when they hear, even if some of them couldn't care less about the people.

But none of them knows how the mind control works. How unbearable the pain Daros can inflict is.

When a knock sounds, I yell for them to come in, not caring

about formalities. In come my guards, Jaku, and Inkga. The latter turns to go, but I tell her to stay and listen if she wants. After all, this might affect her as well as me.

Jaku takes the note first, his mouth set in a grim line. He hands it to the next guard, who reads it, hands it down the line, and says, "We should put a better watch on this room."

Eldim, who reads the note next says, "It'd be a better idea to keep the queen out of this room. Away from the danger."

"Best not let any changes happen. It's what they want," a guard I don't recognize says.

Stird looks at it next. "We have to do what they say, to keep the queen safe"

"We need more guards around the queen," Julina says

As they argue, I watch them carefully, wondering if what they are really thinking is the same as what's coming out of their mouths, or if one of them is a traitor.

"Are you going to give into their demands?" Jem asks when silence fills the room.

I know she doesn't want me to. She wants me to keep her as Head Advisor. "I don't know yet," I say.

"Whatever you decide, your safety is paramount. If they can put this on your pillow, then we need to have more guards on you."

Jem's changed so much. I thought one of the guards would say that, not her. She's come a long way from the snide girl I first knew. "There were no guards in the room while I was away."

"Still, we can't take chances."

"What are you going to do? Have them watch me as I sleep?"

"If that's what it takes to keep you alive, then we're going to do it."

"I can't sleep with people watching me." I can, but they don't need to know that. It's the principal of the thing.

"I'm sorry, Your Majesty, but Jem is right. In this, I must insist," Jaku adds.

I snort. "You're not sorry at all."

He almost smiles.

But really, what am I going to do about this? "I need a way to contact the kidnappers and find out if he's really alive. They had him long enough to take the ring, but without anything this time, who's to say he didn't escape? Or die? I want to demand some evidence of Daros."

"That would be a wise move, Your Highness," Jem says.

"But how will we go about it?" Eldim asks.

I don't want to say it, but I have a feeling at least one person around me is a traitor. Maybe more. It's a sobering thought. And the man they want as my new Head Advisor? Tido Sauvers? How does he fit into this all? Is he their puppet, or do they have some other devious plan?

"I'll write a note, leave it on my pillow, and exit the room." I say it as matter of fact as I can. "Spread the word to everyone you can that I left a note for Daros in my room, and that we won't disturb it until morning."

It wouldn't be the first time I had danger cross where I sleep. Not even close.

"Absolutely not," Jaku says. "I will not bring threats closer to where you live, eat, and sleep."

I shrug. "I won't be in the room at the time, and this isn't up for debate."

"I don't know how I feel about the idea," Jem says. "But we all know if she wants to do it, she will."

"Thank you." I'm not sure I'm grateful.

"Let's get to it, then," Eldim says.

"Absolutely. Inkga, get me a quill and paper please," I say.

She nods and gets the things from the drawer.

"Thank you," I say.

She hands me what I asked for, along with a book for writing on. I put the book under the paper and write my note. It takes longer than I'd like and not as pretty of handwriting, but I feels it's something I must do myself.

I WILL ACQUIESCE to your request. When I have proof Nash Zorris is alive and well. Furthermore, I want guarantees that he will be kept safe. Until then, I will not do as you wish. ~Queen Ryn

THEY'D BETTER FIND this and do what I say.

I hand the note to Inkga. "Put this on my pillow."

"Yes, Your Majesty."

She disappears into my bedroom.

Once she returns, I say, "I will sleep somewhere else for the night." Hopefully my changing rooms like this doesn't give the staff fits.

"Yes, Your Majesty," echoes through the room.

"And if the note disappears, I want this room searched for a hidden passage. We must find it and not let them use it against us."

"Consider it done," Jaku says.

"Let's head out, then."

My guards surround me as I leave the room. "Inkga," I say, "Do you know where I can stay for the night?"

"I do."

I follow her, not certain what will happen. I want to tell them to leave me alone, but I'm afraid Jaku is going to make them watch me sleep. I don't care for that and could order them away, but at the same time, I wonder if they're needed.

On one hand, it would be comforting to have the guards there while I sleep. On the other, it'd remind me too much of my life with Daros—always controlled, always watched, always told what to do.

I don't want my life to go back to that.

The room on the first floor they lead me to is not as lavish as the one they had me in before, but it is preferable. We believe it has no secret passages, but there's no way to be certain. There's no gold or silver or a sitting room. Just a peaceful little bed and a single window.

Jaku orders a few men stationed outside the window. He leaves Julina in my room and assigns the rest of the guards outside.

I change into a night gown Inkga brought and hold the doll the girl gave me. Thankfully, she also got my daggers from under my pillow. I'd be fine without them because I have the ones stashed on me, but I like having extras.

"Thank you, Inkga," I say.

"I wish there was more I could do for you, Your Majesty."

"You do enough." My voice is soft, for once—something she taught me.

I crawl into bed, trying my best to ignore Julina.

"Goodnight, Your Majesty."

"Goodnight, Inkga and Julina."

CHAPTER 28

SLEEP ISN'T easy under the supervision of Julina, but there's more keeping me away. I'm too worried. Too restless.

I want my idea to work, but I have no way of telling if it will before morning. Finally, in the middle of the night, I get up and exercise. It's familiar and soothing. Julina doesn't react, though I wonder what she thinks about it.

When the first rays of morning come, I'm dressed in a pants-and-shirt outfit and immediately leave the room.

"Is there any news?" I ask the servant waiting in the hall.

"We have no news yet, but we've all been avoiding that area like the plague."

"Good." Now for it to have worked.

I head toward my rooms with my guards in tow. On the way there, I find myself pinching my fingers together. I force myself to stop. Tension still ricochets through my body.

Will Daros have given me something else of Nash's? Will he have responded at all? Maybe he didn't even get my note. There are many outcomes. I shouldn't bother to worry about it until I know, but the thoughts come anyway.

Jaku is waiting outside my rooms. "I thought you'd be here soon."

"Do you ever sleep?" I ask.

"About as much as you do."

I raise an eyebrow.

"I'm going to check your rooms, and you can proceed if it's safe. Afet, with me." He goes inside, sword drawn, and Afet follows.

I force myself to hold still and not give into those tiny tics that want to manifest themselves. The men are gone much longer than I expected, but there's no cry for help. No sounds of fighting.

I give in and tap my foot on the carpet. It's quiet enough that no one should notice. Still, time passes. I'm getting ready to shout out for them, when Jaku appears in the doorway.

"It's clear, and there's a note on your pillow." His face is grim.

I rush past him, going straight toward my bed. I can tell it's a different note than the one I left. There's no seal on this one. What's more, there's a dagger next to it, stabbing deep into the stuffing of my pillow. I ignore it and go for the note. With shaking hands, I open it, and a lock of short brown hair falls into my palm.

Nash's hair.

THIS IS *your only confirmation that we have Nash. If you ask for another, it will be a toe. Now, trade out your Head Advisor.*

I SWALLOW against the bile rising in my throat. I should have known Daros would turn this back on Nash. I'll never do that again if it could mean one of his appendages.

I hand the note to Jaku, but keep the hair tucked tightly in my fist. Is it even his? The color looks right, but it could be just about anyone's.

Jaku scowls. "We're moving you."

"Why? They could get to any other room as easily."

"You don't know that."

"Someone entered the palace and reached my rooms without being spotted." I lower my voice. "There's a traitor in our midst. Someone helping with Nash."

It could very well be Jaku himself.

"I know what you're thinking." He gives me a look.

I shrug.

"It's not me."

"Just what anyone would say."

"My actions will convince you."

A good way to test him would be to say there's another note on my pillow, have him or me hide under the bed, and have one of us catch whoever is coming to pick up the note. I suggest as much."You are not hiding under the bed. Not only is it unbefitting a queen, it's much too dangerous," he says when I suggest it.

I want to argue, but there's no sense in it. "What about you or someone else you trust, who's highly trained?"

"I'll do it myself and speak of the plot to no one else. I'll make sure word is spread again."

"Tonight?"

He nods.

"Very well."

"Now, what are you going to do?" Jaku asks.

"I'm going to make Tido Sauver my Head Advisor." Whoever he is.

"You're going to give in to their demands?"

I smile. "I am. It's easy enough to ignore the advice of my Head Advisor and listen to Jem, who will still be around as a lady-in-waiting. And I know him to be a friend of my enemy, so there'll be lots of chances for me to question him."

"Jem won't be around as much as a Head Advisor, though."

"It'll be enough. The real question is, why would they want to change my Head Advisor when they know I won't listen to him?"

Jaku shakes his head. "I don't know."

I tap my finger on my lips. "It might make me seem weaker in front of the people—changing things so quickly. I can't think of what else they'd be trying to accomplish. Unless..."

"Unless what? I don't like that look on your face."

I'm not sure I should say it aloud, but if Jaku is trying to help me, he should know my thoughts. If he's not trying to help me, than he'd probably guess them anyway. "They are putting Tido in so when someone kills me, he will reign until there is a new queen. So they'll have the next ruler under their thumb."

Jaku's scowl is fierce. "I don't like the sound of that."

"Didn't think you would. But what do you think?"

"That you're right on target with your guess." He sheathes his sword. "I wouldn't put it past Daros to do that very thing. It sickens me to think how very evil he is."

And I used to be one of them.

Granted, not by choice, but I was there. Doing Daros's bidding. And I'm still doing it.

CHAPTER 29

"BRING ME TIDO SAUVER." I am in my sitting room with Stird in the corner and more guards in the hallway and outside the window.

Inkga curtseys. "Yes, Your Majesty."

As she leaves the room, I think of how very much I don't want to do this. I don't want another reason for people to go after my life. Though better mine than Nash's, I assume if I'm gone, so will he be.

I try not to dwell on it. Instead, I ask Stird, "How long have you been a guard?"

"About fifteen years now."

"Have you a family?"

He nods. "I do. My parents live in Indell. My wife works in the kitchens here, so we're able to see each other frequently."

"Do you have any children?"

"Unfortunately, we haven't been blessed with any."

"Siblings?"

"If you'll forgive me, Your Majesty, I should be focusing on my job. I don't want anything to happen to you on my watch."

I wave away his concerns. "It won't. I can take care of myself, and there are guards out there everywhere." And I want something to distract me from my thoughts. They're far too dark and depressing.

"I don't have any siblings."

"Do you enjoy your work here?"

"I do."

Inkga enters, and Stird's face relaxes. He's relieved not to have to talk to me. I try not to take offense.

"Tido Sauver, Your Majesty," Inkga says.

He enters with a bow and a smile.

"To what do I owe this honor, Your Highness?" He's not what I expected. A small man, barely rounded enough to belong in court. His eyes are open and honest—not that I trust them—and his brown hair is longer than is fashionable, reaching his shoulders.

"I..." Wish I didn't have to name him my Head Advisor. He might be the nicest guy around, though he's either under Daros's control or vying to control the government after I'm murdered. Either way, I just want Nash back.

"Yes, Your Majesty?" he prods.

No more dawdling. "I am appointing you my new Head Advisor."

He bows his head, and I can't read his expression. "I would be most honored by the position, Your Highness."

Might as well give him busywork. Nash did some of that too, but I actually listened to what he had to say. This man won't receive the same courtesy. "You will arrange for a council meeting, where I will let everyone know of your new appointment," I say.

"Yes, Your Majesty."

Egh. "You don't have to *Your Highness* and *Your Majesty* me so much."

"But it is my honor, Your—"

"No," I snap. "Do not use them so much."

"As you request."

I grit my teeth.

When I add nothing further, he says, "I'll go set up that council meeting now."

I nod, not trusting myself to speak.

Once he leaves the room, I give a glance at Stird. "What did you think of him?"

"I'm not paid to have opinions." He leaves off an honorific.

Finally, someone paying attention.

"You are, when I ask you to have one."

"Very well. He seems eager to please."

"My thoughts as well." And I wonder what he's hiding.

"I want you to look into him for me—his family, his business, everything about him. I want to know all his secrets."

"Consider it done. I'll start as soon as I'm released from guard duty."

"Get someone else to guard me. I want you on this now."

He nods, and another guard is brought in to take his place. Hopefully, he'll have answers about Tido soon.

Within the hour, I'm sitting before the council, trying not to cringe at what I have to do. It's impossible to avoid. "Thank you all for meeting with me on such short notice. I wanted you to know I'm changing my Head Advisor to Tido Sauver."

A few eyebrows are raised, but there are no protests.

"Forgive me for asking, Your Majesty," Mina says, "but why are you changing Head Advisors so quickly? You barely appointed Jem. Has she been a problem?"

"No. She's been fine. I'm moving her back to being one of my ladies-in-waiting." I debate whether or not I should tell them. It's no secret, but I'm afraid they'll act poorly. Might as well get it over with. Then they'll know how much they want to trust my new Head Advisors for themselves. "I was asked to appoint Tido as my new Head Advisor in order to keep Nash alive."

There's a gasp beside me.

I don't bother glancing at Tido. He's either faking it or not. A gasp doesn't change that.

"Do you think it's wise to give into more demands?" Monkia asks.

"Whether it's wise or not, it's done." I keep my tone even, though I don't feel it.

"This is unacceptable," Kada says. "You can't go appointing whomever you want to keep one man alive."

I have to wonder if Inkga thinks the same way as her mother. "I am the queen, I'll appoint whomever I want, whenever I want, for whatever reason I want."

Silence drips down from the ceiling, covering me in the stares of the shocked council members. It doesn't last long.

"Even if you are the queen," Timit says, "you need to take advice from the council."

Hearing such a thought come from Timit surprises me. He's right. Normally I would listen to them on this, but with Nash's life on the line and his family counting on me, I can't.

"You would be wise to do so," Sidle adds quietly.

The rest of my council isn't so whisper soft. They yell and shout. I hear them, but in the end, I have to go with what I feel is right. I know not to listen to Tido, and I know how to protect my own life. That has to be enough.

And with every request I give into, it's less and less likely I'll ever see Nash again.

CHAPTER 30

"The artist is here to paint your picture, my lady," Jem says as soon as she enters my sitting room.

I leave with her, my guards in tow. "I can't believe I agreed to this when there's so much else going on."

"You need to be remembered."

Before I die and they have to do a painting of me then. Of course, then they'd just do one anyway. Inkga has me all dolled up, with a crown on and a fancy cream dress. She says I look fitting for a portrait, but I feel too done up.

As we walk, I dare myself to ask Jem, "Are you upset at me for letting you go as my Head Advisor?"

She's silent so long, I don't think she's going to answer. Then— "I know why you did it."

"But you don't agree with it?"

"My job as your Head Advisor is over. I'm now a simple lady-in-waiting."

"Who can offer her opinion."

"Can I, Your Majesty?"

"Of course." Not saying I'll follow it.

"Then, if you must know, I think your giving into the demands sets a bad precedent. I think you're making foolish choices, not based on what's best for the country."

Ouch. "I understand."

"We're here." She points to a room, and I enter.

There is a painter in one corner, as evidenced by the giant easel beside her and the paintbrush in her hand. In the other corner is a velvet chair. My ladies-in-waiting are scattered throughout the rest of the room. The room's only window is near the painter.

Everyone curtseys, and I tell them to rise before I take my seat. Then they all sit, except for the painter who gives me directions. "Turn your head to the left. That's right. And your knees over here. You're sitting up straight—good. Keep that up. I'll work as fast as I can, Your Majesty, but this will take some time and more than one visit."

I don't respond. If I did, it would be a biting remark she doesn't deserve. Whoever thought the queens needed to be painted was silly. The First Queen wasn't painted while she was alive.

Of course, people have forgotten about her.

Not that I want to be remembered.

There's so much I could be doing instead of sitting here. Namely, I'd like to be out, looking for Nash. Wilric still has no information for me. The leads are turning up empty. Whatever Daros has planned, he's keeping Nash well-hidden.

At least my ladies-in-waiting are here to keep me company. I can strike discussing certain items with them off my list of duties for the day. "We're glad to have you back with us, Jem," Inyi says. "As good as your temporary position was, we missed you."

Lots of *oh yes* and *very much so* come from the other ladies-in-waiting, some sounding more sincere than others.

Jem smiles as if they all speak from the heart. "Thank you. What news do you have from home, Pina?"

My youngest lady-in-waiting beams. "My parents are pleased

with how much I've been helping the queen. They said they can't wait to hear all the stories I have after I'm released."

I hadn't thought about the honor it would give them to help me. I thought it was just their job. "When will you be released?"

She makes a tiny *O* shape with her mouth and looks down. Her response is quiet. "After you are no longer queen, Your Highness."

When I'm dead. No wonder the poor girl looks out of sorts. "We'll hope you're at the palace, gathering stories for a long time, then."

She darts her gaze to me, widening her eyes. "Thank you, Your Majesty."

I wave. "Please, don't add the honorific. If you're going to call me anything when we're together, call me *Ryn*."

"Thank you... Ryn." My name is so soft, I almost don't hear it.

"Your Highness, I must ask that you hold as still as possible," the painter says.

I work not to grit my teeth. I hate holding still. At least it gives me a reason to participate less as the talk turns to fashion. I listen to them chat about it, but I don't have much to add. I don't care for the conversation until they start discussing about whether or not they should start dressing like me.

"It would be a bad idea to move away from tradition," Lipla says.

"But it would honor our queen if we dressed like her." Inyi sneaks me a small smile.

I grin back, glad someone is on my side.

"I agree," Pina adds.

"Do any of you have beaus?" I ask, to turn the conversation away from me, though it reminds me of Nash. The talk stops dead silent. "What did I say?"

"Ladies-in-waiting aren't allowed to court anyone until after they are released from service," Jem says.

"Oh." I think of all they're giving up. Of Benala, the oldest, who never got the chance to have a family. Of Pina, who's so young and has her whole life ahead of her, and will be a lady-in-waiting for a long time if I have anything to say about it. "I'm sorry."

"Don't be," Freza says. "It's the way things have always been. The queen can't touch. Rules for us aren't that strict, but we're not to have relations either. We knew that when we went into training to be ladies-in-waiting."

That doesn't mean I have to like it.

"That cream dress is very becoming, Your—Ryn," Inyi says.

I glance down at it. Does she mean it? I wasn't so sure when I saw it in the mirror—too gaudy—but then, their tastes are different than mine.

"She's right," Freza says. "It brings out the creaminess of your complexion."

It is the first time they've paid me a compliment. Maybe they do mean it. "Thank you."

"Where did you get it?" Suyla asks.

"I'm not sure. I think my Head Servant, Inkga, designed it."

Oohs and *aahs* sound throughout the room.

"I didn't know she had that sort of talent," Inyi says. "You must tell her how wonderful a job she did."

"I will. She'll be glad to hear it."

The talk returns to fashion, though I listen to it more than before. They are less inane than I thought they were. I see an intelligence in them, even if they're talking about clothes.

I never enjoyed being with a group of people before.

It almost makes sitting here worth it.

CHAPTER 31

STIRD MEETS me in my sitting room.

"You have a report for me?"

"Yes. Tido has very little family to speak of. Just a father. Everyone else died of Alamca a few years ago."

The disease that came with the drought. "Poruah class, then?"

He nods. "As far as I can tell, he has no association with Daros."

"I hear a *but* in those words."

"But his father is deep in debt. I think he could be swayed to do whatever someone wanted if they either held the debt over him or paid off the debt for him."

Money can do a lot to a person's morals. "Find any connection between who holds his father's debt and Daros?"

"None, but that doesn't mean it's not there."

Hmm. "How did he come to be at the palace if he was a Poru-ah?" I don't have anything against them being at the palace. It's just that most of the council are Kurah.

"Worked his way up like others have, such as Monkia. He started out as a stable boy, worked his way up to a footman, where he became friends with one of he advisors. Eventually, that advisor needed more help in his office and requested Tido to help him."

"Adviser to which department?"

"Head of Staff."

Makes sense that he'd advise in a staff capacity since he was working that type of job. "Very well. Thank you for your report. Get some rest."

He gives a curt bow and heads out of the room.

There's much to think about, but little time to do so. Unfortunately, it's dinner time, with others instead of in my room. As much as I'd like to skip it, I need to show what little strength I can.

On the way, I think of what to do with Tido. Or rather, what not to do about him. I'll have to be extra vigilant to make certain he isn't made ruler over my people.

I take my place at the head of the table, and a plate is put before me. Succulent roast duck. It reminds me of the time I ate duck with Nash. I don't know whether to throw it across the room or stick a dagger in it.

Instead, I cut a dainty bite and place it in my mouth. While it's stuck there, the council members and members of court eat. It's annoying that they had to wait for me, and now I'm stuck trying to eat in front of them. I'd much rather take a meal in my room, where I can force it down without an audience.

But no. Affairs of the state can't be ignored, even when Nash is missing.

My heart hurts for him. Rages for the unfairness of it all. And here I am, enjoying a dinner party, when he's probably starving. But Daros needed me to be fit enough to do my job as an assassin. He has no such constraints with Nash. It's doubtful he cares if Nash can even move.

I put my fork down. I can't do this.

"Is everything all right, Your Majesty?" Jem asks. She's down a ways, on my left.

I give her a smile I hope doesn't look too forced. "I'm fine."

She gives a heavy blink like she doesn't believe me, but lets it go.

The chatter around me is inane, but I try to participate. I am the queen. My voice needs to be heard.

"These dirty peasants keep asking for more and more," a fat man with a squat nose and far apart eyes says.

"They ask for more because they need more." My grip on my fork is tight.

"*Need more*," a woman with long eyelashes says from across the table. "All they ever do is need things."

"Don't we all?" I ask.

"You're the one who raised their taxes," Squat Nose says. "You should be on our side, not theirs."

Either word hasn't gotten out about why I changed taxes again, or he's baiting me. Either way, I don't like it. "I won't put up with talk against the poor at this table. They need our help and consideration, not our condemnation."

The table goes quiet. Even the chatter clears at the other end of the banquet hall. I may have spoken too loudly.

"We all have respect for the Poruah," Jem says, saving me.

"We just respect ourselves too," Tido says, from my left.

I thought he would care about the Poruah since he was one previously. I have an urge to whip out my dagger and stab it on the table, between his fingers. Instead, I give him a sour smile. "Does respecting yourself include blackmailing your way into a high position?"

I stab my smallest dagger into the table next to his hand. He jerks back. My satisfaction is tainted by a faint feeling of guilt. Maybe I shouldn't have gone so far, but it's too late to change that now. Despite that, eating is a little easier now that I spat out what bugged me, and the rest of them follow my lead.

Really, Daros can't have been so stupid to think I'd listen to a Head Advisor assigned by him. Unless that's what his next note is going to demand—that I follow the words of this imbecile.

The meal winds down, and people start talking again, this time in whispers. Apparently, I am to be feared, if not respected.

That's fine; I've given them no reason to respect me.

I don't even respect myself.

My end of the table stays subdued, except for my Head Advisor, who slurps and gulps his food in a most atrocious manner. Maybe the man doesn't realize he's being used. Either way, it's like having Ranen all over again, only without the hostility. But maybe that counts for something, though I don't want it to. Not with Daros in control.

When I finish my duck and vegetables, I realize everyone around me has been done for a while. They continued to eat scraps because I wasn't done. Jem's probably internally seething at my not noticing others. Oh well.

There are still mounds of food on the table, just not on people's plates. Who knows what plans they have for it? I can change the waste of food. Daros might not want me to let the Poruah have money, but I can give them food.

I call the nearest servant over. "See that the rest of this food is delivered to the poorest families in the city."

"Yes, Your Majesty."

The servant snaps her fingers, and other servants rush to clear the table. Small talk remains while they do so, though I don't involve myself. Things like which painters are the best, whom to hire to have the best sculptures done, what is the newest place to buy furs, and who has the finest wines.

At least some of the market shops will have patrons.

A hush fills the room as a servant brings me the Mortum Tura. I feel more like splashing it on these inane people than drinking it. The First Queen said it had magic in it, but what good is it if it can't help me locate and save Nash?

I shove the thoughts away. They'll get me nowhere.

"Thank you for joining me this evening." My voice rings out across the room. I meet the gazes of those gathered. A few hang on my words, but most look bored and fidget with their finger-nails or linen napkins.

I press forward, anyway. "As you know, the taxes have changed a lot in the past several weeks. I regret that I've made our economy so jumpy. I will strive to do what I can to remedy that in the future." If only I had complete control, and Nash's life didn't hang in the balance. "While you have a tax break from the govern-ment, I would highly encourage you to consider your spending. Think about using it to help the Poruah and the Medi. The working class. You speak of buying things like paintings and wines. Those are fine, but while you're out making your purchases, please consider giving coin to the poor. To patron those in the market selling wares you wouldn't normally buy. By supporting them, we will all benefit."

A few say, "hear, hear," but nearly all the people remain silent. I'm not to be a popular queen with anyone.

I grasp the chalice by the stem and tilt the cup back. As soon as the liquid touches my lips, a warmth fills me. By the time I've drank it all, heat runs through me like a familiar echo. As that diminishes, I'm curious about what the familiar feeling is.

Whatever it is, it won't bring me closer to Nash.

After replacing the chalice, I stand, and the rest of the room follows suit. I nod and exit the room, my guards attending me. I don't know what it is about this night that has me so out of sorts.

A hot, woozy feeling bubbles inside me, stifled, yet bursting.

I'm only too grateful to return to my rooms. Inkga is waiting for me.

"How did the dinner go, Your Majesty?" she asks as I sit in front of her.

She takes off my crown and sets it to the side, to be taken to the royal treasury. My neck and head immediately feel lighter. Freer.

"I should wear a lighter crown next time," I say.

"There are several tiaras available that might suit you. No one has worn them in a long time, but you could get away with it."

I put my elbows on the vanity and my head in my hands. "The weight of the crown isn't as bad as the weight of the people. I don't know how to lead under normal circumstances, and definitely not when Nash has been taken hostage."

"You do better than you think."

I lean back so she can unpin my short locks. "It's kind of you to say."

"It's not kind. It's honest. You need that more than my kindness."

That's probably true. "Thank you."

"That's what friends are for."

Friends.

My eyes burn. I close them and hide them behind my fingers. She'll realize a few tears escaped, but it makes me feel better.

I regain control of myself and stay silent while she brushes my hair. When she's finished, I pull on my night gown and climb into bed.

"Do you need anything else, Your Highness?" she asks.

"Yes, Inkga. I do."

"What is it?"

"I would prefer if you wouldn't use a title for me when we're alone. You can call me *Ryn*."

She hesitates. "All right, Ryn. Goodnight."

"Goodnight, Inkga."

She takes the crown and leaves the room. A moment later, Julina replaces her.

"You know, it's really hard to sleep with you watching me," I say.

"Forgive me, Your Majesty. It's my job."

"I understand. I just wish things were different."

"Don't we all?"

I'm so tired I drift off with those words ringing through my head.

CHAPTER 32

THE FIRST QUEEN *jumps forward with vivid clarity. My talks with her felt real before, but now they feel hyper-aware.*

"It's the Mortum Tura," I say. "It's making the dreams more lifelike."

"Very good." *She brushes the front of her green dress like there's something on it, but like always, it's perfect.* "It will connect us more."

"Will it help me learn magic?"

"It will give you magic, but you won't know how to use it. You must discover that for yourself."

"Can't you teach me?" *There has to be a way to quickly imbue magic into an object I can use to save Nash.*

"You've been thinking a lot about this. I wish it was as easy as your thoughts, but I must teach you the ways of being queen. Magic is not included. You'll have to do that on your own time."

"But magic can make me a better queen."

She lifts her eyebrows. "How so?"

"Because I can use it to help the people."

"Right now, you only want to use it to help yourself. That's a dangerous thing."

"I want to help Nash."

"And in turn, make yourself feel better."

I cross my arms, trying not to pout. I'm better than that. "If I can save Nash, couldn't I help my people in other ways?"

"Magic is a dangerous thing, not to be taken lightly. Too many have given into its call of greed."

"It makes you greedy? How?"

"Through its power. Just like I didn't want power-desperate queens, so I don't want you to be overcome with greed-inducing magic."

I think about that a moment. "Once, a servant told me Deedra became sad and cruel. That all queens do. Am I doomed to become this way?"

"Only if you let the power go to your head—if you cut me out of your life and go for your wants instead of the needs of your people."

Which I've done twice, for Nash and his family. I push the thought aside for now. "How can I cut you out of my life? You're here most of the time when I sleep."

"Doesn't mean you have to listen to me. If you recall, you did a fairly good job of shutting me out when we first met, even if you still spoke with me."

I do recall. I wish I opened up to her sooner and let her assist me.

"There's still more you need to open up with and let me help. I can only do so much if you don't share things with me."

I purse my lips.

"You can be upset with me all you want. It doesn't change the facts. I can assist you with so many things if you let me."

"Can you find Nash?"

"You need to let him go."

I clench my teeth. There's no reason to let Daros go on torturing him.

"Except that you need to do what's best for the country and people."

She's right. "I can't handle knowing what they're doing to him."

"Same thing they did to you?" Her head is cocked to one side.

I don't want to talk about it.

"You never do."

I hate that she can read my thoughts, but I don't even care that she read that one.

"It's part of the deal. I help you—I can read your thoughts. It's not something I can turn off."

"What did people think of you when you were their leader?" I ask, to change the subject.

"I know what you're doing."

I shrug.

"To answer your question, some people liked me, and some hated me. It's the way of being queen."

"Did they like you or hate you for good reason?"

"Depends on whom you ask."

What type of queen was she? What rules did she make? What lives did she change, for better or worse? "How long were you the queen before you put yourself into the Mortum Tura?"

"Long enough to know what's best for the people is not always what they want."

That was no answer.

"Now you know how it feels."

I scrunch my nose.

"You show too much of your feelings for a queen."

"It's just you and me. What does it matter? You know my thoughts, anyway."

"Most of them, not all. You keep so much hidden. Besides, now is a good practice for later."

I want to argue, but it would prove her point that I show too much emotion by getting upset over it.

"Very good. You're learning. But our time is running short. You need to remember what I say. Your country—your people—come first."

It's hard to remember that when Nash is being tortured.

I wake with my hand on my throat, as if my own hands are against me.

The First Queen said that going for my wants instead of the

needs of my people would leave me power hungry and cruel. Is that what I'm doing, following the will of Daros? Keeping Nash above all else?

Is that making me a bad ruler? Obviously, yes. I've known this, but thinking it so bluntly makes me sick.

CHAPTER 33

THE FIRST THING I do is talk to Jaku alone. I'm armed, in case he is the traitor, but I'm beginning to trust him. "What happened last night?" I ask.

"No one came."

"How can that be? You and I were the only ones who knew it was a trap."

"My only guess is someone is watching your room and saw me go inside."

I growl in frustration. This is not the answer I wanted. I wanted to catch Daros and be done with this. Of course he would probably send someone else in his place, but that person would hopefully have led us to him.

I excuse Jaku and think. As much as I want to change, I worry I'm making the wrong choice. Nash is first in my life. My people should be first in my country. How do I make the two work together?

I'm not sure I can.

My stomach revolts. I breathe through my mouth to contain myself.

A knock sounds and a servant enters to remind me it's time for a meeting with my ladies-in-waiting. I go to them, and they get straight to talking, but it's hard to pay attention.

"Your Majesty?" Jem asks. "Are you all right?"

"I'm fine. Continue."

"We were wondering how we can be of service, my lady," Inyi says.

What can they do? What can anyone do?

There's a low hum of noise I can't pinpoint, but I ignore it. "Tell me, what was discussed between the ladies-in-waiting and other queens?" I'm still not sure I understand what their use is. I've had a couple decent conversations with them, but nothing groundbreaking.

"The words exchanged between previous queens and their ladies-in-waiting are unknown," Suyla says. "What goes on between the queen and her ladies is kept secret."

And then the queen passes away, and the ladies try for the Mortum Tura, either to become the next queen or to die. "Then how do you know what to discuss with me?"

"We were taught to follow the lead of the queen." Suyla's fingers drum on her skirts like they aren't used to being idle.

I shouldn't have taken away their sewing projects, but they drove me crazy with their constant handwork.

The buzz grows louder. "I know what you can do for me. See what that noise is."

Suyla's eyes grow wide. "Me?"

"Yes, you. I want to know what that racket is."

She stands with a scowl on her face. "Yes, Your Majesty."

The rest of the ladies-in-waiting watch her go out before turning their focus back to me. What do I say to them? That I want them to leave me in peace to get some sleep? That I want to rush around searching for Nash? Probably something more practical. I open my mouth to speak when the door bursts open. Suyla is there with Afet, and she's huffing for breath.

Afet says, "There's an attempted attack on you right now. We have to go."

I jump to my feet, daggers drawn. I hurry after him, but my ladies-in-waiting remain in the room. Three other guards wait with their swords drawn.

"Come on," I yell at the ladies.

They follow, faces pale. We make quite the chain, with Afet leading the way, guards surrounding me and my ladies-in-waiting trailing after.

I don't know where we're going. We head upstairs to a part of the palace I'm not as familiar with. Afet takes us through hallway after hallway until we reach a wall with armor decorating it. Afet pulls the helmet open and twists something inside it. The wall swings open to reveal a small room, barely big enough for all of us.

Afet ushers me in before entering himself. Soon, we're all crowded in—all twelve of my ladies-in-waiting, four guards, and I tucked in the corner behind everyone. The guards surround me, except for Afet, who closes the door. I think he stays beside it, but it's so dark, it's hard to tell. The only light coming in is from the lines of the secret door going back to the hallway.

"Are we safe here?" one of my ladies-in-waiting says in a shaky voice.

"We're fine." Jem sounds more certain. "They're after the queen, anyway, not us. We need to protect her, but they won't come directly after us."

"I should have trained you to fight." Especially if the attackers get past my guards. Let's hope it doesn't come to that.

My daggers are still out, though held close to my body, so as not to accidentally cut one of my guards.

For far too long, all is silent.

"When do we know it's safe to come out?" I ask.

No one answers.

This is ridiculous. "Are you sure anyone is even after me? There doesn't seem to be anything happening."

"There have been riots." Afet's voice comes from where I last saw him by the door. "Not a lot, but enough to raise concerns." That explains the noise. "A couple of people infiltrated the castle with the intent to do you harm. Because there were more than one, I think the best course of action is to wait here a while. We don't want to go out there only to find someone else is still after you."

"And they don't know I'm here?"

"Until now, nobody knew about this place except me," Afet says. "At least as far as I know."

"Which guards are here?"

"Stird here." His voice comes from directly to my right.

"Eldim." In front of me.

"Julina." Somewhere close by.

At least I know them all. Being stuck in this room is stifling enough without adding unfamiliar people to the list.

And stifling it is. It's hot, air growing muggier by the minute. Flashbacks hit me of being stuck in similar circumstances, except instead of being surrounded by people in the dark, it would be glass and nails, some of which I couldn't keep from digging into me.

If I could do that for hours on end, I can do this. No problem. My ladies-in-waiting... I can't vouch for. This is probably worse than torture for them.

"What were the crowds rioting for?" I ask.

Silence.

"What were they rioting for?" My voice is firmer this time.

"They're upset about taxes," Afet replies with the sound of reluctance.

Taxes. The Poruah and maybe some Medi, then. The ones I should be helping but have disgraced because of Nash. I knew it was going to be this, but wanted it to be different despite the odds. "What should I do?"

"If you really want to know, Your Majesty," Jem says, making me wish I could see her, "I think that you should stick to your promise about taxes. I know it's hard when your old Head Advisor is suffering, but you can't put one person before your people."

Nash would say the same thing.

What have I sacrificed on his behalf?

Too much.

Nash would be disappointed in me. Let's face it—I'm disappointed with myself. I need to fix this, though doing so means I will lose Nash. My eyes fill with tears that quickly make their way down my cheeks. I'm grateful for the dark; no one can see me falling apart. What good it does to cry, I don't know, but I can't stop it. Can't fight the daggers embedded in my heart.

It will be better, anyway. Nash won't have to endure anymore. They'll kill him, and the torture will be over. Death will betray me once again by taking Nash's life.

The tears come harder. Fierce. Torturous themselves.

It's like my eyes are bleeding.

My heart's being ripped out.

I take three steadying breaths, the same technique I always use, to deal with Daros. The tears subside, but my heart still feels as if it's been shredded.

Did the others notice my breakdown? As quiet as I tried to be, I'm certain they did. It's too small of a room for them not to, even if it's dark. Then again, maybe they thought it was a lady-in-waiting. Queens don't cry.

Except this queen does, especially if it's over Nash.

I take a deep breath and say, "Let's leave this room and go talk to the people."

"We can't leave," Afet says. "Forgive me, Your Majesty, but someone is trying to kill you."

"Only because of what I've done with taxes. I can fix that. Right now."

"I must protest. We can't know that they'll stop coming after you. Things have changed so much, there's no telling that they won't change again."

"So we're going to stay in this room for the next year?" I ask.

"Only until it's safe." He sounds sure, but I don't buy it.

I can't.

I have to believe I can give my people better, and that they'll accept it. "We are going out, and I'm changing taxes. I'll tell them what's happened. Jem, will you arrange a meeting in the throne room?"

"Yes, Your Majesty." I may be wrong, but it almost sounds like there was a note of pride in her voice. I've never known her to sound so upbeat.

"Afet, open the door." I use a commanding tone.

But we remain in darkness.

"Afet?"

"I'm sorry, Your Majesty, Jaku says your safety comes above all else. Are you certain this is what you need to do?"

"I am. You can go get more guards if you want, but I refuse to stay hidden in here."

"Julina, will you go get more guards for me?" he asks.

"I will."

There's a shuffle of movement, and then the hidden door opens. Julina is highlighted in the light coming in. She disappears out into the hall, the door shutting after her. I realize I'm still gripping my daggers, and I slide them back into their sheaths with a *snick*.

The moment I do so, the point of a blade is at my throat, and Stird says, "Don't move."

CHAPTER 34

I SWALLOW, accidentally pressing the blade harder into my throat. It doesn't feel like blood is drawn. "What do you want?"

"What's going on?" Afet asks.

"Everyone quiet and don't move, or I'll hurt the queen," Stird says.

There's a sharp inhale from someone.

"What? Why would you do that? Calm down," a guard says.

"Shut up. Shut up! If any of you speaks again, I will go through with it. Queen Ryn, you will not change the taxes." Stird's knife presses harder into my skin.

"Fine. I won't."

"I doubt that." He pushes the blade deeper into my skin. It stings.

"You've never killed anyone in cold blood before, have you?" I have to keep him distracted while I go for my dagger with my left hand, the one farthest from him. Have to keep him from hearing it slip out of its sheath.

"I..." His voice shakes with that one short word. If only the door remained open, so I could see him and read him better.

"As I guessed. It's harder than you thought it'd be, isn't it?" I rest my hand on the hilt of my dagger, but I don't dare pull it out without some type of noise to block the sound.

If I could see his expression right now it would help. Know what he's thinking. Understand why he's so hesitant, so I can lean on that. Instead I'm stuck guessing.

"Leave the taxes alone." Stird's words come out as a yell.

I keep my voice calm. Controlled. Soft. "I can leave them alone for now, but you have to give me information. Why are you doing this?"

He jams in the blade hard enough that blood trickles down my neck. My heart takes on a furious pace. My nerves are stretched taut. How am I going to get out of this?

"You won't. You'll change them, and you can't. You can't." His voice breaks on that last word.

"Why not? What is Daros holding against you?"

The pressure against my neck is gone, and there's a clatter on the floor. My blade is out, even as I listen to Stird cry.

I've never heard a grown man bawling like this before. A thick, heavy sound, like his heart has been torn from his chest. What on all of my blades could have caused him such grief? A failed assassination attempt doesn't seem enough.

The grief isn't enough to make me keep my dagger away from his own throat. "Don't move."

A sob rips from him.

"Afet, would you let in some light?" I ask.

"Not until Julina gets back with more guards," he says, but sounds uncertain.

"Someone just tried to kill me in this blasted hidden room. I think you can open the door."

"Are you hurt, Your Majesty?" Afet asks.

"No. Just open the blasted door."

Enough light peeks into the room to let me see Stird's crumpled face. He's in a lot of pain, and I've done nothing more than hold a blade to his throat. All my ladies-in-waiting are cramped in the other corner, the guards blocking them from us. Afet steps toward us, but I hold up a hand.

"What has you so distraught?" I ask Stird.

"My parents." His grief crushes his words. "Daros has my parents."

My mouth drops for him. No wonder he tried to kill me. I'm surprised he didn't go through with it. Would I have, if I was in his position? It's difficult to say since I never knew my parents, but it's likely.

"What is he doing with your parents?" I keep my voice soft and ease up my blade, though I don't withdraw it from his neck.

"He said I needed to make certain you went along with the demands he sent you, or he would kill my parents."

Stird clearly cares for his parents. Is there a way to save both him and them? Not that I'll ever be able to trust him again. How many other guards could Daros or someone else get to in such a way? "Do you know where Daros is holding them?"

He nods—a shaky thing. "I've seen them every day. I demanded to, knowing what Daros is like. Wanted to make certain they weren't being hurt."

Hope bubbles up in me. "Is Nash with them?"

"No. I haven't seen or heard where he's being kept."

And just like that, all my hopes are smashed. I bite my lip, trying to pull myself together. This isn't about me. This is about Stird. "When are you supposed to go to them again?"

"Tonight, when I get off work."

"Is Daros there when you meet with them?"

"No. I've never seen him. It's always one or more of his men." His answers are sure, but his voice wobbles.

"How many men are there over your parents?"

"Why are you asking so many questions?" he asks.

I don't hesitate. "I want to help."

"Oh, Your Majesty." He drops to the floor on his knees, clasping his hands together before him, and I allow my blade to fall back enough that he has room. I can't be too cautious around someone with so much to lose. "Thank you. Thank you. I'd forever be in your debt if you saved them."

Until they were captured again. "How many men are over your parents?"

"Five, Your Highness."

I could handle them on my own as long as Daros didn't show up. I doubt Jaku or Afet would go for it, though. "Where are they held?"

"In an upper-class house near the palace, Your Majesty. I'll do anything to save them. Anything at all."

That much is evident, except killing me since he couldn't bring himself to go through with it. "Could you get away with bringing men with you, or do they watch the outside?"

"They don't often look outside, but I can't put my parent's lives in the hands of *not often*."

"So we need to sneak everyone else in while you make certain your parents are safe." I tap my blade against my fingernails.

"There's a back way," he says. "I think I could keep them distracted long enough for men to come in through that entrance."

I want to go. "Afet?"

"Yes, Your Majesty?"

"Organize a group to go with Stird to rescue his parents. I believe I should go with them," I say.

There's a long, drawn-out sigh. "Do you think that's the safest plan, Your Highness?" Afet says.

"You'd be willing to go?" Stird's voice is the calmest it's been since we started talking.

"I would like to. And Afet, I can do this without risking myself."

"How are you going to do that? Forgive me, but no matter what you do, it won't be safe. The people need you. We can't be thrown back into the chaos of not having a ruler. Especially with

Tido in charge should anything happen to you, if I may be so bold to say."

He's right. I ache to do what I know would help. "Fine. But I want this taken care of."

"I'll personally make certain it is, Your Majesty."

Stird is crying again. "Thank you, thank you, thank you, my lady. I will never again give into anything against you. I'll make certain I always come to you first before anyone else."

Not sure how to respond that he's going to be in huge trouble after we get his parents, I tell Afet, "Get Wilric. I want him joining you as soon as he can, even if he can't make it until after everything's over." If I can't be there, he's the next best thing.

"As soon as Julina returns, I'll make it happen."

We sit in silence, which is horridly awkward. I keep my weapon out and pull out a second. One can never be too careful when there's a dissuaded would-be assassin sitting on the floor next to you. Not that I'm worried about him anymore since I said I'll save his parents like he wants me to. But I do wonder who else is against me, whether by choice or by force.

Who wants to assassinate me?

I wouldn't have guessed Stird would betray me. I didn't think he was on my side—just that he was not against me.

Time passes much too slow, but eventually Julina shows up. "I've got two dozen guards with me."

It takes me a moment to remember why so many—she doesn't know what's going on with Stird.

Afet takes care of everything for me. "Julina, I have a special task for you." He explains what happened and sends her off to find Wilric.

"Stird, you go with her," I say. "Make certain you make a good plan for rescuing your parents. You'll only have one shot at this."

"Yes, Your Majesty. Thank you."

Together, Julina and Stird take off.

As for me... I still want to go forward with my plan, but I wish there was some other way to save Nash and my people.

But I can't do both.

"I'm going to announce to the people that I'm returning the taxes to how they should be."

Afet gives out orders, quickly seeing my ladies-in-waiting out and surrounding both them and me with guards. And though I keep my blades out, ready to defend myself, my thoughts are haunted by what I'm going to do.

May Nash forgive me.

CHAPTER 35

THERE'S one thing I have to do before I fix the taxes—tell Nash's family. I ask my ladies-in-waiting, "Do you have any clothes I could change into that would make me less conspicuous?"

"I have something," Benala, the oldest of my ladies-in-waiting, says.

"Take me to your room."

She leads the way. "It will be a little big on you but should suit your purpose, Your Majesty."

"Do you have a cloak to go with it?"

"I do."

We get to her rooms with my escorts in tow, and I hurry and change. Indeed, it requires some extra padding, but in the end, we get it to fit and add a cloak. We move out of the palace through a secret door on the side. Sadly, unless we scale the wall, where people could see us, the only way out of this mess is through the crowd of people who don't seem very happy with me. My only chance is if they don't recognize me. If they do…well, it's trouble.

I'm doing something very stupid. I don't know why I'm risking so much for Nash's mother other than because she deserves to know this from me. More than anyone else, she deserves to know.

"Do you think this is wise, my lady?" Afet whispers.

"Not at all. Let's do this."

Looking resigned, he nods, and we head out as a group. As we get closer to the crowd, I realize my mistake. I'm dressed as a middle class woman among a bunch of guards. I don't look as if I belong with them or with the crowd. It's too late now, though. Several of the people in the crowd seem to have spotted us.

They don't pay us any attention, thank my blades. Still, my nerves are taut as we move closer to the group and toward the portcullis.

The people don't seem to care that a group of soldiers is walking by. I don't see why they should; there are many more out here than I thought there would be. Yet, when we make it through the opening with no problem, I'm immensely grateful.

We hurry down the street, which is more deserted than the last time I went this way. It's cooler than before, too, like even the weather knows something is wrong.

I hesitate outside Nash's house, not sure I want to go through with this. How do I tell a mother I'm going to do something that will lead to her son's death?

I don't.

I take a step back.

The door opens, and Slipa smiles when she sees me. "I thought I heard someone out here. Please, come in."

I find myself following her in, wishing I had different news. That everything was different.

She invites me to sit on her couch, and then does so herself. "I can see whatever brought you here is weighing heavy on your mind, Your Majesty. Go ahead and tell me about it. I'm ready."

"I still don't know where Nash is." I pause longer than I should.

"Is that all? I was afraid you were coming here to tell me that you found him, but he was dead." She gives a shaky smile.

How do I tell her?

Her face falls. "He is dead, isn't he?"

I must be brave. "We haven't discovered that he is, but I've made a decision, and I had to let you know." I swallow to clear the pain from my throat. "I can't give into the kidnappers any longer. I can't let them control the country, even if it means losing Nash."

Before she lowers her eyes, they're filled with tears. She brushes them away. "I'm glad Belta and Lanay were gone for this news. I don't know how I'll tell them. They look up to him so much, especially since my husband died. He's taken care of us. Fed us. Kept a roof over our heads. Warned us of danger. Given us everything we have. He's a friend, a brother, a father figure to the girls. He loves us, and we love him. How are we ever going to get over this?"

"I'm so sorry I have to do this."

Her head darts up to look at me then. "No. Don't you apologize. It's not your fault. You are doing what you need to for the sake of this country. Never feel bad about that. Never."

It's hard not to. It feels so much like my fault.

She tilts her head. "How well do you know him? I know he was your Head Advisor, but did you know him as a person?"

"Not as well as I'd like, but hopefully more than I think." I hesitate. Maybe now isn't the time, but I can't think of another when I will have this opportunity. I need to get back to the palace. To the people. For just one more moment, I want to be me. "Would you tell me more about him?"

She studies me. Really searches for something, thought I don't know what. She opens her mouth, then closes it again with a shake over her head. "He was always a kind boy. Rescued birds when they fell out of their nest. Helped stray cats out of trees. When his sisters were harassed once, by a neighborhood boy, he beat the boy up. At the time I scolded him, but really, the kid needed a good thrashing. He was many years older than the girls, and I wanted to give him a good swat myself. Of course, I ended up giving Nash that swat for fighting when he shouldn't.

"It only made sense when he went into the guard. He fought

hard for the side of good. If you excuse my saying so, he had a difficult time with the last queen. He still vowed to protect her but didn't agree with many of the things she did. He didn't know how to act with her. Do you choose your conscience and what ideals it upholds, or do you pick your loyalty to the crown?"

"Did he talk to you about it often?" I ask, thrilled to be getting so much information about Nash, but wishing that it wasn't happening under these circumstances.

"As often as he could get away, he would come home, though it's hard to come all the way out here. Usually once a week, on leave day. He would spend time with his friends too, but always spent time with us first. He was even more valiant in coming after his father passed away."

I wonder how his father died, but it isn't the time to ask. Not when she's about to lose her son too.

"Oh, I could talk about him for hours. A mother doesn't have favorites, but if I did, it'd be him. Maybe because he was my only boy. I don't know. He's always had such a good heart and a kind soul. Made me want to be more like him, instead of the other way around."

"If you'll excuse me for interrupting—Your Majesty, ma'am— I'd like to say how fine of a guard and advisor Nash was. What a great person he is," Afet says.

I have to hold my emotions in tight, so they don't come roiling out.

"I'm glad you think so," Slipa says. "Can I get you some tea? Food? Anything?"

I shake my head. I should eat something, to be polite, but my throat is too locked up, and my stomach doesn't feel like eating anything. "Thank you, but no. We should be on our way. I need to tell the people I'm fixing the taxes. For good, this time."

She nods. "He'd want that." Her voice grows smaller. "No matter the cost."

She stands, more slowly than she moved before. It's my fault she lost the bounce in her step—my fault her son is going to die—but there's no way I can continue on like I have been. It's not fair to anyone.

"Thank you for bringing me the news yourself, Your Majesty," she says.

"I'm just sorry it wasn't better news."

"It's not your fault, dear. If you forgive me for saying so, I'd hug you right now if it weren't against the law."

My eyes and nose burn, but there's nothing I can do about it. I can't risk her life by letting her hug me. I made it all this way without losing it. Now shouldn't be the time.

"Thank you." My voice is small, but my heart feels big. "That means more to me than I can say."

"You're a good queen. Your heart is in the right place."

Unable to speak, I nod, and we finally leave.

The guards surround me, making it look like I happen to be in the center of our group. It doesn't make a difference since we see no one else.

"You did a brave thing," Afet says. "She needed to hear what you had to say and needed to let out the words she did. Nash would be happy with what you did."

"It's not enough, but it was something."

"You need to give yourself more credit. What you did back there was big to Slipa."

"And she's all that matters now. Thank you. I'll keep that in mind. How long have you known Nash?"

"Since he was twelve. Like his mother, I always admired and respected him. It's not every day you meet a man like him."

"No. No, it's not."

I think about that the entire way back to the palace.

CHAPTER 36

SOMETHING CLIMBS its way through me, swirling around my insides as we walk toward the throne room. I wish I knew what it is.

My guards are flanking me, and there are more ahead. Afet and Eldim stay close. How will this affect them? Will my changing the taxes yet again have a backlash on them, not just me? It's hard to say. I haven't a clue how the people are going to react.

We see no signs of people in the halls. Not even the typical servant or two. So much for someone looking to take my life. Of course, I did send word ahead to have the people meet me in the throne room. Perhaps my assassins are biding their time there.

When we get to the back door of the throne room, I hesitate to give any orders. What situation am I putting us into? Are these guards going to lose their lives? Am I?

Better me than someone else.

Maybe I should have listened to Afet and stayed hidden, but I can't handle doing so when I can appease the people, even if it means losing the man I care about.

I stumble over nothing and fall straight to the floor. No doubt one of my guards could have caught me, but it would mean their death. I can't touch anyone. You'd think I wouldn't care, after a lifetime of only touches of the wicked kind, but I find myself yearning for something soft and kind, if a bit calloused. Nash.

Why am I letting my thoughts stray at a time like this?

Because I'd rather deal with them than what must come.

"Your Majesty, are you all right?" Eldim's voice comes from above me.

"Fine." Just fine.

I pick myself off the floor.

I'd rather have stayed there.

I nod to the door, and the guard closest to it opens it. They hurry through until it's my turn. I slink through the opening, taking in everything around me.

It's almost too much. The room is filled with people. And the noise... it's fierce and angry.

I have done my people wrong.

It's time to fix that.

My guards surround me on the dais and flow out into the room in front of me as I try not to think of Nash.

Anything but him.

"My people." My voice rings out clear and strong against the crowd. They simmer down, though they don't quiet all the way. "I have done something I'm ashamed of. I have raised taxes for those I care about the most—the poor and the needy. I will be honest with you. I have done so because my Head Advisor was kidnapped, and threats were sent that if I didn't tax you more, there would be deadly consequences for him."

The noise dies. I swallow, trying to find a way to say what must be said. "I am sorry for doing this to you. I only wanted him to survive. But I know that can't be. I have done you wrong in my attempt to save him. I won't ask for your forgiveness. I don't deserve it. But I will return the laws to the way things should be. The Poruah will have little to no taxes, the Medi class, very few taxes, and those who can afford it most will take the brunt of the taxes. I'm sorry anyone has to pay any at all. We are doing what we can to minimize government spending so we don't have to charge as much."

So many words, and none of them the ones that will bring him back.

The people respond well, though. A cheer rises up. I take a closer look at them than I did before. They are wearing tattered clothes, and dirt smudges their gaunt cheeks.

The Poruah.

How many were here before, wanting to take my life, and how many gathered after they heard I would be speaking to them? It doesn't matter. They're here, and they heard. Maybe now the threats on my life will ease. Though I didn't do this for my safety or that my guards can pay me less attention. If anything, they're more vigilant than ever—faces stern, hands on hilts, eyes taking in everything.

Their vigilance makes me proud.

"What if you change your mind again?" someone from the crowd yells.

"Right," another calls out.

"She could do it."

"We're never safe with her as queen."

An odd sensation is all the warning I get. I duck, only to feel the wind on my skin as an arrow whips by. My neck stings, but not enough to get in the way of my action.

I fling myself to the side, daggers in hands. I bump into a guard and jerk away from him, hoping I didn't injure him.

"This way, Your Majesty," Eldim calls out.

The guards have formed a pathway straight out of the room. I follow it.

I can tell the crowd is restless when I glance back. Some people come after me, some stand still, and others race for the other end of the room, where the exit is. I focus my attention on the path before me.

"Duck," Afet yells.

I throw myself to the ground, ignoring the sting to the front of me where I land. Someone groans in pain. I get to my feet, keeping my head ducked down. A guard in front of me has an arrow coming out of his shoulder.

An arrow meant for me. I stand still, staring at it.

"Get out of here," Eldim hollers.

I press forward, diving through the doorway. Several guards run in after me, and Afet slams the door closed. I get to my feet, feeling foolish for overreaching for the floor, and make for a jog away from the fray.

Why are the people trying to kill me now? I'm giving them what they want. Or is it someone sent by Daros?

"Over here, Your Majesty," Eldim says.

I follow him up a flight of stairs, though my thoughts are scattered. Of course they tried to kill me. I can't be consistent; it's going to be a long time before I can get anyone to trust me again.

I'm a killer of dreams.

Everyone's dreams.

Even when I try to do the right thing, I end up doing wrong.

I try to shut my brain down as we move through the palace. We come to a desolate area. There's no sound except that of our feet padding and our hard breathing as we jog. We slow to a fast walk. I glance in rooms we pass and find sheets draped over the furniture.

At least someone listened to me and closed up part of the palace.

After we've gone a ways in, Eldim darts into one of the rooms, I go in, and the rest of the guards follow.

"This should have us in a good place to wait out the crisis, Your Majesty," Eldim says.

After what happened with Stird, I don't want to trust him, but I'm not sure I have any other choice right now. Not if I'm to be a queen with guards.

The room is like the others, with giant white sheets covering everything. It looks like there is a couch and several chairs. Unsurprisingly, the cream walls are decorated with paintings of Valcora. I feel like I've seen enough of it through the paintings that I'd recognize places if I were to travel the country. Which maybe I should. Maybe people would like me more outside this city.

"This should be fine." I pull a drape off the couch and take a seat, though I feel more like taking someone down. I need to cool off. To think about what happened.

The people attacked me.

Not an assassin, *the people*.

I've got to do a better job at this queen thing. I don't know what else to do, though. For starters, having Nash back at my side would help. I wince. Daros has probably gotten word I've changed the taxes back and is likely taking care of him for good. How am I going to deal with this?

I shy away from these forbidden thoughts.

Maybe it wasn't the people. Maybe it was Daros again. It has to be.

I focus on what needs to happen. "We just wait this out?" I ask.

Eldim and Afet share a look. Afet is the one who braves speaking. "If they simmer down, we'll be fine, but if they don't, we might have to move you out of the city."

"It's not like they can take the job away from me." Then I remember. "They'll just kill me."

"We won't let that happen, my lady," Eldim says.

I glance around at the soldiers in the room. There's a dozen of them, carefully stationed around the room. Several stand by the doors, and two by each window—though staying out of direct view. These men are willing to give their lives for me. How am I returning the favor? By getting them shot.

The man that was hit with the arrow. "Where's the injured guard?" I ask.

"He got left behind." Eldim says matter-of-factly.

"How did that happen?" I jump to my feet and head toward the door. "We have to help him."

"Forgive me, Your Majesty," Afet says. "If we go back for him, we'll be bringing him more danger than if we leave him there. The other guards will see to him."

They're right, although that doesn't make me feel better.

I pace.

There's so much going on; my mind is overwhelmed. One thing is certain—I've got to stop making people put their lives on the line because of me.

CHAPTER 37

I worry about so many people, my thoughts flitter from one person to the next. The worst part is that I'm stuck doing nothing while they are in danger. It's not fair.

It's been hours since we found shelter in this room. Eldim sent a guard to check if things were calmed down or if it was still too dangerous to go out. That was a while ago. Is he ever coming back?

"We should go," I say to no one in particular.

Eldim crosses the room toward me. "Your Majesty, I'm afraid it isn't safe."

"I can handle whatever comes."

"I know you're skilled, but even the most skilled person can't take on an entire crowd."

True. That doesn't mean I want to stay here. "We can't wait forever. We need to know what's going on."

"We will. It takes time."

I'm sick of waiting. My people are probably rioting. The guard who was shot is probably dead. Stird's parents are probably being tortured in front of him. And Nash... he's probably dead.

I clutch the armrest of the chair to keep from crying out. Why did I allow my thoughts to wander there? I have to get myself under control.

The door bursts open, and my guards are on the move. Two of them flash their swords on the person entering.

It's the guard sent to find out information.

"Stand down," Eldim says.

They put away their swords, and the guard comes forward to face Eldim, Afet, and me. "Things have calmed down, Your Majesty."

"So we can go." I move forward, but he doesn't. "What's wrong?" I ask.

"It's not pretty. The people are still upset. I think it'd be wise if we stayed put for the night."

Stay put? Not when there's so much that needs to be done. But can I ignore advice I should have been listening to all along? "What about the council? Are they safe? The ladies-in-waiting? And Inkga. I'd like here here with me."

"All of them are safe, Your Majesty. You're the only one in danger."

That's a relief. "Go get Inkga, and see if you can find Wilric. He should be back with Stird by now. I also need to speak with the other guards who went with Stird as soon as they return. I need to know his parents are safe."

"Forgive me, Your Majesty," Eldim says.

"I'm beginning to hate those words." I pierce him with a glare.

He nods but pushes on. "It's just that the more people we have coming and going through here, the more people are likely to find out this is where you are hiding."

"I don't care about my own safety over these things I've requested of you. They need to be taken care of."

"Can you at least wait until morning?" Afet's voice is soft.

"No. I need them taken care of now. Especially Stird."

The guard before me bows. "I'll do what I can to get everyone here discreetly, Your Majesty."

He's out of the room before any more protests can go up—one thing to be thankful for. I drum my fingers on my leg and tap my foot. Normally, I wouldn't allow such movements in front of others, but it doesn't seem to matter right now.

"A game of Nako, Your Majesty?" Eldim asks.

"Is there one in here?"

"There is." He pulls out the board from under a white sheet.

I grin. "This would be perfect." I've been practicing ever since I lost to Nash in what little free time I have with different guards.

He opens the box and pulls out the pieces. Soon we are set up and playing. I win three out of four games while the night edges in. It's a good way to pass the time, though it feels fruitless with what's going on outside these walls.

In the middle of the fifth game, there's a knock on the door, and cautiously, two guards open it, weapons ready. I can't help but be glad to see a familiar face.

"Your Majesty." Inkga runs over to me, large bag in hand, and kneels on the ground next to me. "Are you all right? I've been so worried since I heard how the crowd was acting."

"Please stand, I'm fine."

She gets off her knees. "The guard said so, but I had to hear it for myself. What did you need me for?"

I can't say the real reason. I just needed a friend in all this chaos, but what excuse can I give? "Why don't you put this room in order so I can spend the night?"

"Consider it done." She takes a dress out her bag. "I also brought something for you to change into."

I look down at the over-sized disguise I'm still wearing. "Thank you, Inkga."

I change and watch Inkga work, trying not to fidget. She does a good job of keeping me company, but it's hard to focus on her words or do anything but wait for what comes next.

"Tell me what you know," I tell Inkga as she flits from one place to the other.

"I'm sorry to say it, but the people are angry with you. The Kurah are upset because of their raised taxes. The Medi and Poruah are upset you keep changing things around, though I heard some say they're grateful you were honest with them about why changes took place like they did. I don't think anyone expected you to explain yourself."

Not even me, if truth be told. "Do you think they'll forgive me?"

"The Medi and Poruah will with time. The Kurah? I don't know. It's hard to say."

She's wiser than I thought. I wish I'd asked for Jem too. I need to reinstate her as my Head Advisor.

Stird walks in the doorway, followed by an older couple and Wilric. I assume the couple are Stird's parents, but I don't get a chance to find out for sure. Wilric walks up to me and says, "I know where they're holding Nash."

CHAPTER 38

"Where is he?" My heart feels as if it will thump right out of my chest. "Is he alive or..." Is it just his body? I gulp past the fear.

"I don't know."

"Then we have to hurry. The longer we take to get him, the more likely they are to kill him." I hop on my feet and head toward the door.

"There's just one problem."

I turn back at the sound of Wilric's voice. "What is it?"

"The reason I came back—I need more guards. There are over fifty men in the house Nash is in."

I give a short, hard gasp. Fifty? That's more than even I can deal with. I round my shoulders. There's no way we'll get him out alive. I straighten.

At least we can get him out, even if it's just his body. I owe him that much.

"What about Stird's parents? How did you get them out?" Maybe we can do the same.

"They were held in a different spot, nearby but less guarded."

Drat. "How did you find out where he is?"

"I did some reconnaissance around the area before we went in. Saw Nash through a window."

I want to ask how he looks, but I don't dare hear the answer. "He's alive?" That will have to suffice.

"I couldn't tell under the circumstances, but I'm certain it was him."

"We're going. Afet, gather as many men as you can get on the sly. We'll do whatever it takes to get him back." Without crossing any more ethical lines, that is. But we will get him back. Even if he's already gone.

I choke back my emotions, struggling to get them under control while Afet leaves the room with a, "Yes, my lady."

Eldim approaches. I know what he's going to say, and I don't want to hear it. "I'm going. There won't be enough men to keep me safe, but I need to be there. Need to do this. Nothing you say will make me change my mind."

He opens his mouth and closes it again. With a bow, he steps out of my way. I head toward the barracks, wondering if I should send his mother a note. She has a right to know what's going on, especially if I don't survive. Problem is I don't want to take time to write a note. The more time we waste, the more likely Daros is to move Nash.

"Inkga?"

"I'm here, Your Majesty." She hurries forward, pushing her way through the group of guards surrounding me. "How can I be of service?"

"I need you to go to Nash's family's house. Tell them what's going on and that I'll do my best to bring him back safely." I can't bring myself to say he'll probably be dead. They'll have some closure at least. We all will.

"Consider it done."

Before I can say anything further, she's commandeered four men from the back of my group and is headed in the opposite direction. I send her good wishes. If only there was more I could do for her. For all of us.

I wish the First Queen was here to reign with her commanding presence, so I'd be even freer to go after Nash. But I'm going to do it anyway. I've done so many stupid things since he was taken. Why not add one more to the list?

Besides, he's calling to me. I can feel it.

Wilric is by my side. I say, "They're going to have a lot of men in there. What else do we need?"

"Just the guards," he says. "If we have enough, we can take him. Your Majesty, I hate to say this, but—"

"I know."

"I have to say it anyway. Once they see us coming, they're unlikely to keep him alive."

"I know." All too well. "We'll have the dark on our side. If we keep as silent as possible…" I'd like to say there's a chance, but really, there's none with Daros in charge.

"We'll do our best."

By the time we make our way to the barracks, a large group of guards is gathered. It would be nice if I had time to change out of my dress, but I don't—not when lives hang in the balance.

There are enough men here to take down Daros. He better be at the same place as Nash.

Wilric gets a report that there are one hundred and three soldiers here. That should do the trick. He leads the group, while Afet and Eldim cushion me in the middle of the soldiers. They were serious about keeping me safe.

If only it was that easy.

We march through the city more quietly than I thought we could. I don't glimpse anyone else out and about, but then being stuck in the middle of the group limits my sights. By the time my gaze reaches them, the people are probably hiding, not understanding that we aren't coming after them.

My people need to know they're safe, but that'll have to wait.

When they realize we didn't attack them, and instead attacked a known culprit, they'll understand. I hope.

We don't make talk on the walk. It's much too fraught with nerves and danger. I grip my daggers like they're an extension of me. For all purposes tonight, they are.

We come to a house that looks like any other in the neighborhood, and the guards surround it. It isn't far from where Daros used to live. To think we were that close to Nash all this time and didn't know it. They hid it well when we were looking. That, or they've been moving him around.

How have they gotten away with having so many men and not being noticed by the neighbors? Daros always had people coming and going, but I never knew how he did it.

Everyone is silent. There's no movement inside. No flickering candlelight. Nothing.

They have to know we are here.

They're staying inside, waiting for us to attack one by one. It's the best way to take out larger numbers, and I wish they came out swinging.

On the signal from Wilric, my men storm the house. The only sound is the clanking of metal and feet moving. Though I have a good number of people on my side around, Afet and Eldim have me hanging back with several other guards.

Why did I come? I'm of no use back here, doing nothing.

Several minutes pass, before I can't take it anymore. "We're going in." I hurry forward, my guards rushing to keep up.

Afet says, "Are you certain it's safe, Your Majesty?"

"Safe enough. We haven't heard a sound since they went in." Which could mean a lot of things.

Eldim opens his mouth like he wants to argue, but shuts it again without saying a word.

Smart man.

We move into the house, Afet going before me and Eldim after, along with the other guards. Plenty of my people are around the house, though. Two are stationed in the first room we enter. It's a big room, bare of furniture. The large window shows the outside, where three of the five moons shine bright.

"Send men to the neighbors," I say. "I want to know if they've noticed any unusual activity here the last few days, and if they know the person or people that live here."

"I'll go," a guard I don't recognize says. Another joins, him and they leave.

It would be strange if nobody had a clue, with fifty men supposedly being here.

I move deeper into the house and find more of the same. Blank walls. Uncovered floors. No furniture. It's like no one has ever lived here—or if they have, it's been a long time.

Footsteps thud down the hall. I pull out my weapons, though it's unlikely to be the enemy, with so many guards about.

Wilric comes into view. He says nothing about my being in the house. "No one's here. There's evidence that Nash might have been here, though."

"What evidence?"

He grimaces. "I'm not sure you should see it."

"Show me." My tone holds no room for not following orders.

With a nod, he leads me past an unused kitchen, down some stairs, and into a basement that has several guards with torches. Flickering in the torchlight in the corner are splashes of crimson.

Blood.

Nash's most likely. And chunks of brown hair the same color as his. That can't be good.

A set of heavy chains hang from the wall, unlocked. And on the opposite wall, a small barred window to the outside.

Where is he? Why didn't they leave his body behind? And where are the fifty men that were supposed to be here?

I brace myself against a wall as I stare at the stains on the dirt floor. This shouldn't have happened.

There's a patter of feet coming down the stairs. It's the guard who went to speak with the neighbors.

"What news do you have?" I ask.

He bows. "They knew something was going on, but thought the neighbors were having lots of parties. Lots of guests. There's been a lot of movement, but they didn't see anyone leave."

"Then where are they?" Better yet, where is Nash?

CHAPTER 39

I PACE THE BASEMENT, seeking an answer that doesn't exist. Most of the men are upstairs, going through things. More likely, waiting for me to be ready to go. But I won't be until I find him, even if it's just his body.

My stomach churns.

Afet, Wilric, Julina, and Eldim are down here with me. Watching. Waiting.

I feel like a bear, trapped in a cage. None of this is doing any good, but the kidnappers can't have disappeared.

Then it hits me. It could be like the palace, with hidden rooms and halls. No wonder no one saw them go out. No wonder they didn't attract enough attention for guards to come crawling all over the place. There has to be a secret way out of this place, and the sooner I find it, the sooner I'll be on Nash's trail.

I move to the closest wall and run my hand over the rough wooden beams. "Look for secret entrances."

I knock on the wood, looking for a hollow sound. There's a solid *thud*, like it's got packed earth behind it. I continue knocking all over the entire wall, high and low. If it's here, I will find it.

Nothing unusual manifests itself. Nothing to make me think I'm on the right track.

But then I think of Daros's secret torture chamber, the one back at his house. The one I was all too familiar with. There has to be something like that here. An exit.

I cross over to the dried blood on the floor. I've been avoiding the area, but I can't any longer. I have to find the way, even if it means facing things I don't want to face. I keep my gaze away from the stains of rust-colored blood and focus on the wall. Bad move. Now that I'm this close, I see more flecks of scarlet.

It was as I feared.

Even in the end, they didn't go easy on him.

Swallowing the rising bile, I knock on the wood. Then knock again. *Hollow.* There's something back there. I just have to reach it. I run my hands against the pieces of wood, pressing against it. There are no lines to indicate where the door might be, and I'm not finding any ways to open it. It's almost like magic, but that can't be. People don't use magic in this country.

So how do I open it?

I search the area again, more thoroughly.

There's a crack that's cleaner than the rest of the wall. I run my finger along it. I find nothing out of the ordinary until there's a small bump of a switch. Heart pounding, I press against the wall the same time as I flick the switch.

The hidden door swings open.

I glance at the long, dark tunnel revealed before us. The others flock around me.

Afet says, "I'm going for backup."

And I'm going forward, no matter how many men I have to fight with only a few guards. No sense waiting when every second the Daros could be getting farther away. I take a torch from someone next to me, pull out my dagger with my other hand, and hurry forward. The others follow me.

The way is dank. Dusty. Filled with cobwebs. Nothing here to indicate anyone's been through lately. Maybe I was wrong.

I bend and let the light shine on the floor.

Red splotches stain the ground. I touch it with the tips of my fingers. Still wet.

For the first time since I came to this house, hope fills me. I wish there was a way to know if it's Nash's or not—to know if he's still alive and if they're taking him to his doom. I will get his body back if nothing else.

I clench my jaw.

Whatever the case may be, I bolt to my feet and run through the passageway as fast as I dare. It tilts downward, going for some distance. I don't bother checking if there's more blood in the passageway. Whether there is or isn't, it doesn't change my destination.

Spider webs tug at my skin. I brush them away with the back of my dagger hand and press forward.

"Maybe we should go back," Eldim says from behind me. "Or send someone else in our place."

"At least let one of us go first," Wilric adds when I don't respond.

"It'll be fine." It has to be. I need it to be. I can't give the kidnappers another minute to get away.

We continue, the path tilting up slightly now. And then we come to a dead end. I hit the dirt wall. Nothing but earth. I try the walls on each side, but they're as solid as the first. What now?

"Any ideas?" I ask.

"Turn back," Afet says.

I ignore him. He has my best interest at heart, but I have to press on. Only there is nowhere to press on to.

I want to punch something, but that wouldn't help me get any closer. There's a light tread of noise. I glance around. It wasn't one of my men. It comes again, louder this time. I look up. Why didn't I think to try above me?

If I try now, though, someone will be waiting for me when I pop up. My guards stare up at the ceiling. They must know to stay quiet, because none of them say a thing despite the continued noise from above.

That noise could be one of the people holding Nash. The thought spurs me forward. I don't care if they're waiting for me or not. If they have Nash and haven't killed him yet, there's a chance I can save him.

It's a small hope, but I grasp onto it.

With a torch still held in one hand and a dagger in the other, I turn sideways and shove on the boards above me. Because they are boards. I don't know how I missed it before. They go flying open.

"We're under attack," a female voice calls above me.

Before our opponents get any farther, I jump up and shove myself over the side, throwing my torch ahead of me and using its flame to drive them away. My right hand takes a cut, but nothing deep. After me, a guard tries to scurry to where I am.

It's dark up here. Once on my feet, I grab my torch again. As soon as I swing it upward, there's a young woman diving for my face.

I block her with my dagger, blood seeping down the back of my hand. She grins like I gave her a prize. A girl after my own heart.

"Are you sure you don't want to fight on my side?" I ask.

"Why? So you can oppress us all with your rules?"

I slash at her with my dagger. "Rules your master told me to enforce. I've only made them as they are because of him."

She sneers. "You know nothing."

My guards storm up the room, attacking others around them. It's tight with bodies and blades. They had better be trained well enough to handle a job such as this.

With a quick thrust, the girl dives in toward me, sword in

hand. I block it, smirking. "I don't, do I? Except how to beat you. Your left side is weak, and your swordsmanship is sloppy."

"Like you would know."

She comes at me, full force. I easily step aside and smash the hilt of my dagger into her head. She falls to the ground.

"I know all when it comes to fighting," I say. With a few more swipes across her head, she finally goes unconscious.

There's plenty more struggling going on—my guards fight people in Medi clothes. It's hard to tell who's going to win at this point. My reinforcements better arrive soon. I whirl my torch around the room, trying to decide who needs my help the most when I spot someone with a shaved head, covered in blood.

Someone I would recognize, no matter what they did to him.

My heart stops.

Nash.

CHAPTER 40

I RUN TOWARD HIM, but a man with a giant sword steps between us.

"Little girl, you better run home to your momma."

I sneer. He has no idea who he's dealing with. Granted, he is big, but not enough to scare me. "You'd better run home to your own momma before I cut off your life," I say.

He shakes his head. Slowly. Like he's stupid.

I throw one of my daggers at him, knowing it'll hit its mark no problem. But he moves faster than I expected a man of his size to. He darts down. I stand and stare. Maybe he's more of a challenge than I first thought.

He comes up, thrusting his sword toward me. I block with my dagger, my heart thudding in my throat. I need to get a gap between us, but I can't lead him to Nash.

We do a dance—me darting in and out of his reach, him following my foot patterns. There's a danger in getting too close, but it's better than taking him to Nash. I manage to slice him on the left arm as I twirl away. He growls but shows no sign of slowing. I swing my torch at him, to force him to keep his distance. He bats at it, almost knocking it from my hand. I give the handle a firm grip to make certain it doesn't slip from my grasp.

As I continue sparring with this huge man, I notice my guards try to reach me, but their combatants get in their way. They don't want me to have help. That's fine.

The sword flashes in my face.

I may need more help than I thought till now.

There's a *clang* as the blade of my dagger hits the metal of the sword. It happens over and over again. I'm losing my area. Soon, I'll be over by the wall, close to Nash. At least I think it's a wall. It's hard to tell.

I have to keep my ground, though. I whip the torch back and forth, near my opponent's face. His lip has a split right down the middle, glistening with saliva. My stomach protests, but there's not time to think on it.

The man grins at me, the split stretching out. I block his sword with my torch and move my dagger toward that split. Before I get there, he jerks back. No easy target. Exactly what I don't want, when Nash is lying on the ground. If he's still alive, he needs attention. And if he's not...

Can't think. Must fight.

I move reflexively, diving in and out, away from danger and in for a strike. I get the tip of the torch on him, but he moves before it can do any real damage. He jumps so far back I'm tempted to run to Nash. But no. I have to finish the man and all other combatants still up, or I won't be able to help Nash properly.

Taking a wild step to the side, to end this fight early, I chuck my torch at my opponent. It hits its mark. The man screams, staggering backward. I keep my attention on him while seeing how everyone else is doing out the corner of my eye.

A guard is next to me, fighting for her life against another burly male. I pull out a dagger and throw it at her attacker's back. There's no time to see if it does its job. My opponent is coming back at me, face contorted with rage.

Maybe throwing that torch was a bad idea.

I pull out yet another dagger as I block the first blow. I move my hands in a fast array of motion. I'm faster than him, but he's got a longer reach. And anger, which is both good and bad in a fight.

He presses in on me, making me wish I fought with longer blades. Then he slumps to the ground.

Wilric stands in his place. He gives me a nod.

With a quick glance around, I find that my guards are holding their own, and many of our opponents have gone down. I could jump in the fray, but it doesn't look like they need me.

I keep the dagger in my right hand, but put the other away as I rush to Nash's side. His eyes are closed.

Is he...?

I grit my teeth against the sudden onslaught of emotion. This is too much to deal with. I glance around the room, to make certain no one's sneaking up on me. My guards are headed this way, but everyone else is tied up or unconscious.

When I look back, Nash's face is ashen. I reach forward, hand shaking. I yank myself back before I can touch him. It doesn't matter if I do or not, his chest isn't moving. Tears pool in my eyes. I knew it would come to this. Knew he wouldn't be able to last.

"What have they done to you?" I whisper.

A tear drops and lands on his skin. I so badly wanted things to turn out differently. To be all right. For Nash not to suffer because of the choices I made.

"I'm so sorry." I want to rest my head against his chest, but I can't touch him. Instead, I cry into my hands. The soundless sob aches through me, but is nothing compared to the agony inside my soul.

"Ryn?" The voice is raspy but familiar.

I pop my eyelids open to find Nash staring at me.

"You're alive." The words jump from me.

"For the moment." It's the most wonderful sound I've ever heard.

"How are you not dead?" I ask.

"I don't know. This feels like heaven, compared to what I've been living through."

I want to take his hands in mine, but don't dare with the guards watching. "I'm so sorry. It's all my fault. I should have done what they told me so you wouldn't suffer."

"We'll talk about it later." Despite his voice cracking, it's so good to hear him. "I want you to know I would do anything to protect you—to protect the crown—even if it meant dying."

"Don't talk like that."

"Can I get some water?"

I turn around to order one of my guards to bring some. They're all focused on Nash and me now. I add fierceness to my words. "Someone go get some water."

I want to do more for Nash. "We need to get you back to the palace."

He closes his eyes with a nod. "There's a lot we need to talk about. My attackers were plotting against you."

"I know." I keep my voice soft.

"Do you know who they are?" Wilric asks, voice soft yet demanding.

Nash coughs. When he gets his breath again, he says, "There was one they called the Hand."

I glance up at Wilric to find his knuckles white from gripping the sword so tight. "Do you know who that is?"

He nods and points to the man I threw my torch at. He's tied up in the corner, barely conscious.

Without a thought, I hurry toward the man. He smirks at me, as though drunk, until he sees my face. Then he tries to scoot back, but there's nowhere for him to go. I grab him by his shirt, fisting my hands up. It takes everything in me not to hit him, even when he's already so beat up.

"Why did you do this?" I demand. "Where's Daros?"

"Who's Daros?" His words slur together.

"You know who he is. The man who's been ordering you around. The one who told you to hurt Nash."

His lips clamp tight together. He's not going to talk.

Rage ripples through me. I want to punch him in the stomach over and over again until he talks. I can't handle him keeping things from me when I'm so close. "Where is Daros?"

His gaze crawls up to meet mine. He must see something of my rage there because he blanches, but still doesn't give in. Wilric puts a foot on his hurt ankle and presses down. The man cries out and yells, "You can't tell him it was me who told you."

"You'll have a lot worse to deal with if you don't tell me everything you know right now."

"It was Ranen."

"Ranen?" What is he talking about? His pain must be making him delirious.

"You don't know." He cringes, as if in pain, which he probably is.

"Know what?" I try not to make my tone harsh. Demanding. But it comes out that way anyway.

"Ranen's the one who had Nash kidnapped. The one who made us torture him."

"No. No, no, nononono." That doesn't make sense. It can't be. "He's been in the dungeon this whole time. He can't be behind the plot."

"He is," the Hand says.

"Could he be, Your Majesty?" Wilric says from somewhere behind me.

I shake my head. "I don't know. Tell us more."

"All I know is what I've been told. Ranen's been in contact with us this whole time, even from the dungeons. There's at least one guard who is loyal to him. Didn't want to let him out yet, though, because he was safe orchestrating it from his cell."

"What about Daros?" I ask.

"He has nothing to do with this."

Ranen was really behind it this whole time? I can't believe it. I let go of the Hand's shirt, and he slumps backward. As I hurry back to Nash, I send instructions to have several of the guards check out the prison.

Wilric is at Nash's side, binding the worst of his injuries.

When I get to them, Nash reaches for me but then stops himself. "I'm so glad you're here."

"I'm glad to finally have made it." I whisper the words and then say more loudly, "Can you walk?"

"Better than being carried."

"Not if you need the assistance. We can get you to the palace." Except that would slow us down, and I'm eager to get back.

He sits up so slowly he might as well stay lying down. Wilric reaches over to help him. I make myself scarce in a corner, to process what the Hand said. Could Ranen be behind this plot? I have no reason not to trust the Hand, but none to trust him, either. I have to find out for myself.

"I have to get back to the dungeon."

Nash gives a humorless laugh. "That's definitely you, Ryn. A few times I thought you were here, but it was my brain playing tricks on me. No, this is you."

Guilt slaps me in the face. I haven't done a great job with him. He needs nurturing kindness right about now, and instead, I'm giving him nothing good. Just more worries and fears.

I get to my feet and let Eldim assist Wilric with Nash. He can stand on his own, but not without grimacing. It's a long way back to the palace to go like this. Part of me wants to go ahead, to get to Ranen and make him pay for what he's done. The other part is frightened to leave Nash again. Even with my guards surrounding him, I don't trust his safety.

I don't trust anything.

I have to stay with him.

But—oh—it hurts to see him like this.

"Be gentler with him," I say. "Can't you see you're hurting him?"

He's got an arm slung over the shoulder of Wilric and another over Eldim's. It's then I notice it and gasp. Nash's pinky-less left hand lays limp.

"What's wrong?" Wilric's sword is out while he continues to hold up Nash.

"It's nothing." I try to erase the sight from my mind.

"She's just surprised I'm so pretty," Nash says.

He really is a sight to behold. Bruises cover him. Dried blood. Who knows what other scars? He's not at all like the man I knew a week ago.

His head lulls forward while he half-walks and is half-carried by Eldim and Wilric. We head out of the building. We never considered this. Just another basement, in a Kurah house, down the street from the one we were at before. The longer we're here, the more guards show up, but they're too late to do any real good.

It doesn't matter. Nash is here, not well but alive.

CHAPTER 41

"Go on ahead and make certain Ranen is in the dungeon and stays put until I get there," I say to Eldim. "I sent guards, but I want you to go too."

"I should stay with you, Your Majesty."

"No. I need to do this myself, but since I can't, you're the next best thing. I'm trusting you to make sure he's there."

He looks as if he wants to argue more, but Wilric says, "We'll take care of Her Majesty. There are enough guards here. I'll make sure nothing happens to her."

Eldim nods, another guard takes his place helping Nash, and he runs off toward the palace. He'll be there long before us and keep an eye on Ranen.

Now that I know the true source of the problem, I can't help but worry about it. How has Ranen managed so much from behind prison bars? And why?

I have to focus on Nash.

I tell the closest guard, "Get Nash's family to the palace."

He nods and hurries away.

"How are you holding up?" I ask Nash.

He grunts.

Not good. I wish there was a way to get him to the palace faster. I need to think of something to distract him. "Did you know I made Jem my Head Advisor while you were gone?"

"You didn't." There's a hint of humor in his voice.

"I certainly did. You'd be surprised how much better we're getting along. I'm beginning to think that she has some good opinions. Some."

He snorts.

"Go ahead and laugh, but all I say is true." I want to ask what they did to him. How he handled it. How he's even still alive. But I can't have that conversation when he's barely dragging himself through the streets. "I did all sorts of things while you were away."

"Like what?" He takes short, gasping breaths.

I want to grab hold of him. "I sat for my portrait. And, would you believe it,my ladies-in-waiting are not as bad as I thought. I enjoyed spending time with them, in fact."

"Things *have* changed," is all he manages to get out.

I continue to talk. About what I said with the girls. About how Stird's parents were captured, but we got them back. About how finding him was thanks to Wilric's hard work.

We come to the palace, and the portcullis is raised for us. I don't worry over how many people are behind us. We go right in.

Inkga is the first person I see. She's not even waiting inside the palace but outside the front doors.

"What do you need, Your Majesty?" she asks before I get to her.

"A healer, as soon as possible."

She gives a curtsy and runs like I want her to. Like I want to.

"Help will be here soon," I tell Nash.

"I'm fine."

I give a slight smile. "Sure, you are."

"Seriously. Now that you saved me, I feel better."

My heart melts a little, but he's not doing as well as he says.

Eldim is not in the dungeon, where he's supposed to be. He's waiting for me inside the doorway. We usher Nash to a nearby seat where he curls in on himself.

My heart thuds against my ribs as I look to Eldim. Why is he here? This can't be good.

"I'm sorry, my lady." His voice is more regretful than I've ever heard it before. "Ranen is gone."

CHAPTER 42

Nash makes a choking sound.

"That can't be," I say, trying to not let myself be distracted to go help Nash. There's nothing I could do for him right now anyway except try to find his captor. "He has to be there. Has to."

"I'm sorry. It's all my fault," Eldim says. "He wasn't there when I arrived, but if I'd gotten here sooner, I might have caught him."

"What about the guards down there and those I sent before?"

"I found them tied up, unconscious."

Is one of them Ranen's man pretending to be captured to stay close to me? I can't trust anyone except a few of my close guards. Maybe. "Did you wake them? Did they know anything?"

"Not a thing. The guards you sent said Ranen was in his cell when they arrived. Next thing they knew, they were being woken by me, with a giant headache."

Fabulous. "What do we do now?" I can't have another criminal on the loose. It's not happening.

I turn around and go right back outside, facing the eighty or so soldiers still hanging around. "Ranen, the old Head Advisor, has gone missing. I want him found and brought to me as soon as possible." When they stare at me, I yell, "*Now.*"

The guards turn back to where they came from, another guard going along and giving them orders. It's likely they'll have just as much luck finding him as they have Daros. This is horrible. I can't believe the predicament.

"Nash, let's go to my rooms. You're rooms aren't secured, and the healer will come see you there." Mostly, I want to be with him. Especially with Ranen on the loose, I can't trust Nash to go to the barracks to be seen by a healer.

Wilric and Afet help him to my rooms, where Nash insists he's fine in a chair in the sitting room instead of going to my bedroom where he can lie down. "It wouldn't be proper," he says.

"Like I care for such things."

He gives me a faint smile, but says nothing further.

Wilric and Afet leave the room, presumably to stand guard outside.

"What happened?" I ask. "How did they capture you?"

"As easily as I snuck into your rooms." Ranen and several burly guards come out from my bedroom, one with a bow pointed directly at Nash.

CHAPTER 43

At least I found Ranen. This is a horrible place to be in, though. I can't handle putting Nash in danger yet again. I stand in front of him to block him from view. Now the arrow is pointed at me, but it doesn't matter. Better me—the one who messes everything up—than Nash, who is good to the core.

I open my mouth to call for Wilric and the other guards, but Ranen stops me. "I wouldn't do that if I were you."

"Why not? Afraid to handle a little fight?"

"I know you better than that. It wouldn't be just a *little fight*. It would be something atrocious."

I give a half-smile. "So you're scared."

He glowers, reminding me of all the reasons I always hated him. "I'm no such thing."

"Then why don't you fight me yourself?" I ask.

"I'm not trained in fighting, like you are. Unlike some uncouth people, my strength lies in words."

"Words are not your specialty, unless you count yelling and throwing a fit as a good thing."

He scowls, and I know I've hit a nerve. One I shouldn't be hitting when his man has an arrow pointed at my heart.

I hit it anyway, grateful to be able to. "So why all this charade, if you could have gotten yourself out of the dungeon long ago?"

"Like I'll ever tell you."

"How did you get in here?"

"Secret tunnel that you'll never find." He grins and snaps his fingers. It's the only warning I get before an arrow is speeding toward me. I duck, but not fast enough. It embeds itself into my left shoulder. Thank goodness or it would have hit Nash. I'm not accustomed to protecting anyone but myself. I break the shaft and pull out my daggers before another arrow is loaded.

I let loose a dagger into the shooter's chest and drop him to the ground. It wasn't a deadly hit, but it should be enough to knock him out for a while.

"You really want to do this?" I ask Ranen.

He grins, a startling expression that sends chills running down my spine. He snaps a second time, and another three men come pouring out of my bedroom before I have time to think about what's happening. I back into Nash, who slides a dagger out of my pocket.

I'm only too happy to let him. He's in no condition to fight, but I can't have him weaponless either. He needs to be able to protect himself. It's my hope that the men will focus on me instead of him, though. Six men I can handle myself, but not when I have him to protect. I don't know how we're both going to get through this alive.

The first man comes for me, sword drawn. I plant a dagger in his arm and whisk another out my boot. As I'm bent down, he hurtles toward me with the second and third men close behind. There's not enough room in this little place to fight so many.

The floor is firm beneath my feet, giving me the confidence I need to win this fight. A fourth man hurtles past me and locks the door to my sitting room. Backup will not be quick in coming.

I scream for help. The locked door won't keep my guards out

for long, though maybe long enough. There's already a thump of something hitting it.

There's no more time to think about it. The three men are on me, barely held at bay by my daggers. Swords flash before my eyes. It's all I can do to keep up with them and stay in front of Nash.

Sweat drips down my face, getting in my eyes, but I can't wipe it away. A blade makes it past my defenses and slices my left arm. I grit my teeth against the pain, ignoring the liquid spilling out onto my arm. I lift it in time to block another sword coming at me.

While they aim for my torso, I've got to do something to get around them. As I block one, I kick one of my opponents in the groin. He drops his sword with a grunt and dives backward.

One down, but four to go—plus Ranen, but he admitted he can't fight. He's not the real threat here; his minions are.

As four blades try to reach me and Nash, I block and whirl, kicking the hand closest to me. The owner yells as I throw both daggers, one right after another, to land in the shoulders of two attackers. There's lots of groaning, but one opponent hasn't been hurt.

The remaining attacker laughs, probably thinking I don't have a weapon to defeat him. I have nothing within reach, but I'll use my body to block him to the last, no matter what it means. I can't let him get to Nash.

He reaches back to swing at me, the blades in my boots too far away. He's going to win, unless I get his sword away from him. It all happens so fast—while he moves his sword forward, Nash calls out, "*Duck.*"

Trusting he isn't doing this to sacrifice himself, I dive to the floor. A whistling is promptly followed by a moan of pain.

I jump for the sword, which my attacker holds loosely in his hand. He doesn't put up much of a fight while I get it. He stumbles back a few paces. When I take him all in, I notice that one of my daggers is sticking out of his chest. Nash got him where he will never be able to do damage to anyone else.

I put the sword I'm holding to Ranen's throat and direct my comment at the nearest attacker. "Tie up the others."

He has one of my daggers sticking out of his shoulder. "You haven't won enough for me to do so."

"Haven't I?" Without warning, I press my blade into his opposite shoulder. He hisses, moving away from me. I turn to the second attacker, the one I kicked in the groin. "Tie up the others."

He glances at Ranen, his face screwed up like he's not ready to stop fighting, but then relaxes his expression into defeat. He rips the curtains and ties up his comrades. I'll deal with him in a moment. First I need to secure Ranen and get the door open so my soldiers can come in. They're pounding on the door, and I wonder how long that's been going on. At this rate, they'll break through it before I can unlock it.

I pull a dagger out of my boot, and swap the sword into my left hand and the dagger into my right. It's more comfortable this way —feels like it's meant to be. "Sit on the floor next to your buddies."

He does so, and though he's not secured yet, I'm much more confident that I can handle all of them.

"Why did you do it? Why make me raise taxes? Why take Nash?"

Ranen sneers. "Because you are unfit to be queen. I wanted the people to be unhappy with you. I made you name Tido your Head Advisor, so I could control him after I sent someone to kill you or had the people do it for me. I want revenge for how you treated me. Nash, the man you care about, will never be himself again."

"Who said I care about him?" How could he possibly know that? Where did I slip up?

"You were wearing his coat when you came to visit me in the dungeons."

I clench my jaw. How could I be so stupid? "How was that telling?"

"I've never seen a queen accept such a thing from a Head Advisor before. Only a fool who cared about him would accept his coat. Besides, you look at him with more kindness than anyone else."

I want to rage at myself for making the mistake that cost so much, but the past can't be changed, only learned from.

I put down my blades. This is it. Fighting's over. I've won, and Ranen is going to be out of our lives. Done torturing people.

There's a burst of movement, and before I can stop him, Ranen is at Nash's throat.

The promise I made myself not to kill flashes through my mind. It's not something easily forgotten, even when the moment is a fast one that seems to somehow last forever. It's either deal with what's happening and live with the consequences, or stop it no matter the cost to me.

It's not a hard choice to make with Nash's life on the line.

I let my dagger go, not stopping to watch where it lands, because I know it's a death blow. What I don't know is if Ranen will be able to move before it kills him. I jump forward, knocking his blade away, but it's already falling from his grasp.

Ranen is dead.

And the promise I made myself not to kill is broken.

CHAPTER 44

IT'S BEEN EIGHT DAYS, and I'm still fretting about not keeping my word. If I can't even keep a promise to myself, how can I keep one to my people? Nash is worth it, but that only makes it so much easier to bear.

"How are you feeling?" I've been asking him that a lot lately.

"Fine. Happy to see you. Better."

I smile. "Good answers."

"I thought so. Now if only we could have more privacy," he whispers.

There are several servants in the palace room I insisted he stay in until he's fully healed, none of which I trust.

"The healer said you needed lots of rest and constant attention, to make certain you didn't regress."

"Can't you give me that?"

I grin. If only I could.

There's a knock. One of the servants answers it. He says, "Nash Zorris's family, Your Majesty."

"Send them in." I'm grateful they're here. They've been around often since I sent word that Nash had been found.

Nash's eyes light up at the sight of them. "Mom."

"Hello, handsome."

He laughs, a dry sound that's not at all his normal self. "There's much debate about that at the moment."

And it's true he doesn't look like himself. Bruises—purple, yellow, and green. Cuts still healing. His hair like prickles on his scalp instead of long locks. Dark circles under his eyes from the lack of sleep because of nightmares. I wish there was something I could do for him, but what? Maybe with magic, but I don't know enough about it. I need to learn more.

"I'll give you some time alone," I say.

"You don't have to go, Your Majesty," Slipa says, but I'm on my feet and out the door.

Outside the room is a retinue of guards. Though Ranen is no longer a threat, no one wants to leave me unguarded. Jaku is with them. He waves me over farther down the hall, but where we can still see my other guards.

"How can I help you, Jaku?" I ask.

"I'm worried over your safety, my lady. Daros is still out there."

Don't I know it? "After everything we've been through, he's nothing but a fly on the wall."

"That may be, but he still presents a danger to you."

"We'll keep a sharp eye out. You've increased the guards around me. I'm certain we'll be fine."

"Be that as it may, I'm recruiting more guards for the general work around the palace. We're increasing security overall."

"Do we have the funds for that?" After all, I lowered the taxes for the Poruah and Medi. I make a mental note to tell them I'll keep my word this time, though it's going to take a lot more than that to make them believe me.

"I went over the budget with Timit," Jaku says.

"I'm sure that was helpful," I say sarcastically.

"He wasn't the most forthcoming, but I did eventually get that we have enough funds to hire another hundred guards if we close down parts of the palace like you previously suggested."

"By all mean, let's do it." I don't know that we need a hundred men, but giving people jobs is better than keeping parts of the palace open.

"I'll get right on it." He bows and leads me back to the group of guards.

How am I going to deal with the Kurah? It's going to take a lot of thought to figure that out. I'll think of something. If not, Nash will help me, though I worry about his state of mind after everything he's been through. But he's tough. Ranen's men may have done a number on him, but he is strong.

Nash's family comes out of the room, and Slipa stops when she sees me. "Thank you for all you've done for my son, Your Majesty."

"I wish I could have spared him all of this."

"No one could have done such a thing. It's not your fault evil exists in the world. You're doing the best you can to fight it."

As we give our goodbyes, I wonder if she's right. Am I doing my best? I feel like I've spent too long giving in to whatever evil wanted. I can't dwell on such thoughts now. I can't change my past, only my future.

I hope my future lies within the room. I enter, and the servants give me a bow. I motion for them to rise, and otherwise ignore them.

Nash grins, and I return it, though it's not his usual one. When I reach his side, I sit on a small stool next to the bed.

And then my smile falters. "Maybe it is time we have some privacy." I turn to the servants. "Leave us."

They curtsy or bow and head out of the room.

"I'd like to think this is going to be a good moment, but I can tell from the look on your face you have something other than *alone time* in mind."

"I'm sorry, Nash. I want to know how bad things were for you —how much they hurt you—so I know how to help."

His gaze skitters to the side. "I don't know. It's not something I like talking about."

"The healer said the same thing, but that you needed to talk about it."

"What about you? Are you going to talk about what it was like for you growing up?"

I clamp my mouth shut. He's got me there. It's not something I want to talk about at all. I'd rather eat garbage.

"Then we don't need to talk about me either."

I sigh. I have to give in, sooner or later. He needs this as much as I do, no matter how little I want to admit it. "Tell you what—I'll ask you a question, and you can ask me one. When one of us gets pushed past where we want to be, we can stop. Sound good?"

"Not really, but I'll go for it. Only if I get to start, though."

I grit my teeth. "Fine."

"I know we're not supposed to, but—," He takes a deep breath, "Will you hold my hand?"

Surprised by his question, I take a moment to respond. "Yes. I'd love to."

I take his hand into mine, feeling the rough callouses that have hardened from his using a sword and other weapons. Despite the hardness, there's a gentleness there as well. Something nice about the way he firmly takes me in his grip. He has a long way to go before he returns to his full strength, but right now I feel like he could take care of me.

"Your turn," he reminds me.

I don't know what to ask after that. "Why don't you go again since that was a question we both wanted answered?"

"Fair enough. Was it like what I went through? Growing up, I mean."

I give his hand a squeeze. I'd rather do that than talk, but he promised he'd answer if I did. "I don't know exactly what you went through, but it was probably a little like that. Daros needed to keep me in somewhat decent shape because I had to stay well enough for him to use as an assassin whenever he wanted, but that didn't change the fact that he loved to torture me. I was his personal torment toy. He'd do with me as he willed, whenever he willed it."

"I'm sorry you had to live through that. No one should."

The words mean more now that I know he's lived through part of it too. Not that I want him knowing what it felt like. More than anything, I wish he never went through something so horrific. "Thank you. If only I hadn't gone through it, but then, it's made me who I am today. I can't complain about that."

"No. I can't say I'd complain about it either. I love you for who you are."

The words swarm in my head, twirling round and around until they reach my heart. "What did you say?" I ask.

"That I can't complain."

"No. After that."

He smiles, soft and sure. "That I love you."

"Even after everything I put you through?"

"What do you mean, *everything you put me through?*"

"I mean the torture you had to endure. The pain and ridicule."

He takes my hand in both of his. "Ryn, that wasn't your fault."

I glance down, trying to tell which hand is whose. His is bruised and bandaged where his pinky used to be, mine thin and strong. "It feels like I caused it."

"But it isn't. I promise you it was Ranen's. He caused all these problems. He was selfish, trying to rule the country in a way he thought he could. He didn't understand you're the rightful queen."

"So he took it out on you." It hurts to say. I glance at his bandage, where he's missing a finger. "When did they take it?"

"Right away."

I don't know if that makes me feel better or worse.

"They didn't like how I wasn't cooperating with them," he said.

"Did you cooperate after that?"

"That's two questions, but no. I never did."

"That reminds me." I reach into my pocket and pull out his father's ring. "This belongs to you."

He slowly picks it up, as if in awe. "I thought it was gone forever. I didn't know why they took it, except to maybe sell it. It's worth a lot of money, but worth more to me as an heirloom that belonged to my father."

"They sent it to me as proof they had you. And then they sent your hair, the second time."

"When they shaved me, I'm assuming."

"I'm sorry. I should have never asked for a sign."

"They didn't scalp me, and hair grows back fast. It'll be fine."

Still, I miss his hair. It was long enough that I would like to let my fingers play in it. To feel the strands between my fingers. But that won't be happening for a while.

He winces.

"Are you all right?"

"Fine. Ready for a nap."

"Should I leave you?"

"No. I want to ask more questions."

"We can continue later, when your body is well rested. Blades know it's hard enough, dealing with this as it is, without adding pain to the mix."

"No. I want to know. With all that's happened, how do you feel about being queen now?"

I'm not sure how to answer. I take my time. "I feel better, though I've betrayed the people. I know I'll have to work hard to regain their trust, but I want to. This needs to happen. I want to have a long life, helping the people as best I can. I'm just not sure how."

"I'll help you however I can."

"Thank you. Now you really need to get some sleep."

"Will you be here when I wake up?" His eyes are already closed, words slurring.

"I'll always be here."

A smile flits across his lips, and then he's out.

I watch his chest rise and fall, wishing I could curl up next to him, but the bed isn't big enough. Plus he'd be killed for it. Seeing him is better than nothing.

I watch his chest rise and fall. I'm so grateful to have him here. To have him back at my side.

I'll make him my Head Advisor again as soon as I'm ready. In the meantime, Jem's temporarily filling in. She knows it's not permanent. Still, I trust her advice more than I did before, when she was a lady-in-waiting.

I close my own eyes, listening to the soft sound of Nash's breath. It's soothing—nice and gentle. I lean back in my chair, grip his good hand, and close my eyes. I could sleep like this for a little while. I have things to do, yes, but they'll wait.

Until one little thought hits me.

Daros's jewel was in Nash's room.

"Nash." I nudge his shoulder. "Nash, wake up. I need to ask you something important."

"Hmmm?"

"Did you see who took you when you were first kidnapped?"

"Mmm."

He's not fully awake. I ask again.

"No. I didn't see them." His words blend together. "They put something over my head, so I couldn't."

"They? There was more than one?"

"Yeah." He yawns. "Two of them wrestled me until they knocked me out. Before I went out, I heard a voice. It was familiar, but I couldn't quite place it."

"Was it—" Do I have to say it? "Daros?"

His eyes flash open, fear shining in them. "It was."

"Daros was in cahoots with Ranen. They were the ones after your life."

"It can't be."

But it is. "Daros is out there. Waiting for me."

ALSO BY JANEAL FALOR

If you enjoyed reading this book, please consider helping the author by leaving a review where you purchased the book and/or on Goodreads. Even a simple one line review helps.

You can sign up to receive notification when Janeal Falor releases a new book at www.janealfalor.com with a Release Notification link on the side bar. Or talk to the author directly at janealfalor@gmail.com

BOOKS BY JANEAL FALOR

Death's Queen Series

Death's Queen (Death's Queen #1)

Death's Betrayal (Death's Queen #2)

Mine Series

Mine to Tarnish (Mine Prequel)

You Are Mine (Mine #1)

Mine to Spell (Mine #2)

Mine to Fear (Mine #3)

Sacrifice of Mine (Mine #4)

Darkening Light

Ever Darkening (Darkening Light #1)

Savage Light (Darkening Light #2)

Elven Princess

Standalone

ACKNOWLEDGMENTS

When writing acknowledgments, I always feel humbled by the amount of talent that helps me make a book what it is. The people who help me are beyond fantastic. I couldn't make my books what they are without them.

I would have to write a whole other book in and of itself to thank Sotia Lazu for all the help she gives me. She is amazingly wonderful and assists me through so much. From the outline to the finished product, this book would not be what it is without her.

Jessie Wolf has wonderful feedback, helpful comments, and tons of grammar finds. Her help is invaluable in making my book the best it can be. A big thanks to Yesenia Vargas for proofreading and catching some continuity errors. You help me feel like I can put my book out into the world.

And most of all, my family. They are incredibly supportive, giving me time to work, listening to my ideas, and help to encourage me. My children are so patient and kind. They are my best supporters, telling everyone about my books. Erik, you are beyond anything words can say. I would scour the Earth to find you. Love you all!

ABOUT THE AUTHOR

Amazon best selling author Janeal Falor lives in Utah with her husband and three children. In her non-writing time she teaches her kids to make silly faces, cooks whatever strikes her fancy, and attempts to cultivate a garden even when half the things she plants die. When it's time for a break she can be found taking a scenic drive with her family or drinking hot chocolate.